"I'm offering yo

wanted."

"You're a few years too late, and that situation was nothing like this one."

"No, it wasn't. Now I have a life to offer you. Now we have a daughter together. Now we just might have another—"

"I think we need to stop talking about what might be and think about what is."

Marsh leaned in on her again, so close that Tory felt his warm breath on her face, so close that the pull of attraction between them seemed a magnetic force, charging the air around them. "What might be *is* what matters. You had my baby once without me. I hate that it happened that way. I'm not going to let it happen that way again. Damn it, I *will* be what I never had—a good father. If you're pregnant, you will marry me...."

Dear Reader,

Silhouette Books publishes many stars in romance fiction, but now we want to make *you* a star! Tell us in 500 words or less how Silhouette makes love come alive for you. Look inside for details of our "Silhouette Makes You A Star" contest—you could win a luxurious weekend in New York!

Reader favorite Gina Wilkins's love comes alive year after year with over sixty Harlequin and Silhouette romances to her credit. Though her first two manuscripts were rejected, she pursued her goal of becoming a writer. And she has this advice to offer to aspiring authors: "First, read everything you can, not just from the romance genre. Study pacing and characterization," Gina says. "Then, forget everything you've read and create something that is your own. Never imitate." Gina's *Bachelor Cop Finally Caught?* is available this month. When a small-town reporter is guilty of loving the police chief from afar and then tries to make a quick getaway, will the busy chief be too busy with the law to notice love?

And don't miss these great romances from Special Edition. In Sherryl Woods's *Courting the Enemy,* a widow who refused to sell her ranch to a longtime archrival has a different plan when it comes to her heart. *Tall, Dark and Difficult* is the only way to describe the handsome former test pilot hero of Patricia Coughlin's latest novel. When Marsh Bravo is reunited with his love and discovers the child he never knew, *The Marriage Agreement* by Christine Rimmer is the only solution! *Her Hand-Picked Family* by Jennifer Mikels is what the heroine discovers when her search for her long-lost sister leads to a few lessons in love. And sparks fly when her mysterious new lover turns out to be her new boss in Jean Brashear's *Millionaire in Disguise!*

Enjoy this month's lineup. And don't forget to look inside for exciting details of the "Silhouette Makes You A Star" contest.

Best,

Karen Taylor Richman,
Senior Editor

Christine Rimmer

THE MARRIAGE AGREEMENT

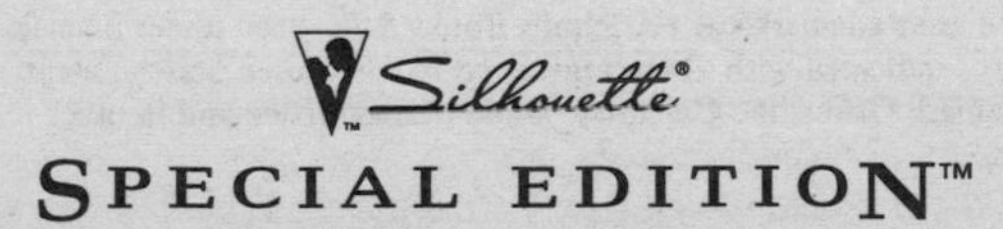

Published by Silhouette Books
America's Publisher of Contemporary Romance

For Barbara Ferris, my e-mail pal,
who loves a good romance, sends me great jokes
and is always checking in just to see how I'm doing.

Thanks, Barb.

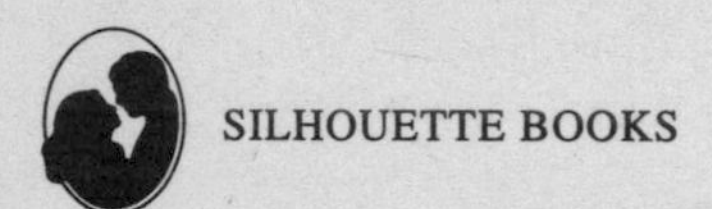

ISBN 0-373-24412-6

THE MARRIAGE AGREEMENT

This edition published by arrangement with Harlequin Books S.A.

Visit Silhouette at www.eHarlequin.com

Printed in U.S.A.

Books by Christine Rimmer

Silhouette Special Edition

Double Dare #646
Slow Larkin's Revenge #698
Earth Angel #719
**Wagered Woman* #794
Born Innocent #833
**Man of the Mountain* #886
**Sweetbriar Summit* #896
**A Home for the Hunter* #908
For the Baby's Sake #925
**Sunshine and the Shadowmaster* #979
**The Man, The Moon and The Marriage Vow* #1010
**No Less Than a Lifetime* #1040
**Honeymoon Hotline* #1063
†*The Nine-Month Marriage* #1148
†*Marriage by Necessity* #1161
†*Practically Married* #1174
**A Hero for Sophie Jones* #1196
Dr. Devastating #1215
Husband in Training #1233
†*Married by Accident* #1250
Cinderella's Big Sky Groom #1280
A Doctor's Vow #1293
†*The Millionaire She Married* #1322
†*The M.D. She* Had *To Marry* #1345
The Tycoon's Instant Daughter #1369
†*The Marriage Agreement* #1412

Silhouette Desire

No Turning Back #418
Call It Fate #458
Temporary Temptress #602
Hard Luck Lady #610
Midsummer Madness #729
Counterfeit Bride #812
Cat's Cradle #940
The Midnight Rider Takes a Bride #1101

Silhouette Books

Fortune's Children
Wife Wanted

**The Taming of Billy Jones*

*The Jones Gang
†Conveniently Yours

CHRISTINE RIMMER

came to her profession the long way around. Before settling down to write about the magic of romance, she'd been an actress, a salesclerk, a janitor, a model, a phone sales representative, a teacher, a waitress, a playwright and an office manager. She insists she never had a problem keeping a job—she was merely gaining "life experience" for her future as a novelist. Christine is grateful not only for the joy she finds in writing, but for what waits when the day's work is through: a man she loves, who loves her right back, and the privilege of watching their children grow and change day to day. She lives with her family in Oklahoma.

THE BRAVOS

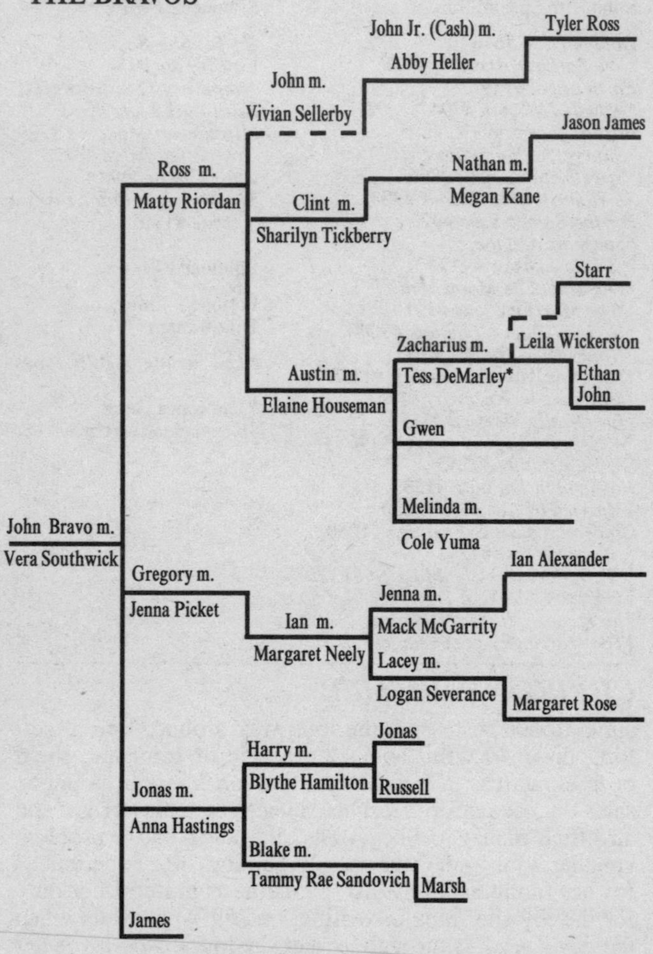

(Broken lines indicate previous marriages)
*One child from a previous marriage: Jobeth

Chapter One

Summoned.

There was no other word for it.

Marsh Bravo had been summoned—by the father he hadn't set eyes on in ten full years, the father he'd thought he'd put behind him as surely and completely as he had the Oklahoma town of his birth. As surely as he had turned his back on Tory.

Tory.

He'd trained himself not to think of her. And he rarely did anymore. There was no point. And besides, even after all these years, just thinking her name caused a tightness in his chest, a pained echo of longing in the vicinity of his heart. Putting Victoria Winningham behind him had not been easy. In fact, it had been the hardest thing he'd ever done.

Leaving his father behind? Well, that had been a

relief, pure and simple. It had been walking away from murder before it had a chance to happen.

On the hospital bed, Blake Bravo stirred. He turned his head, opened sunken, unfocused eyes. Eyes of a gray so pale they seemed otherworldly. Eyes that would have looked just right staring out of the head of a mad wolf.

Marsh had his mother's dark-brown eyes. He'd always been glad of that. The last thing he needed was to see his father's eyes staring back at him every time he looked in the mirror.

The old man on the bed sucked in a wheezing breath. They had him on oxygen. He raised a veined, mottled hand with IV lines taped to the back of it and batted at the plastic tubing attached to his nose, letting his hand drop to the sheet again before he'd managed to dislodge anything.

The old man…

It was more than a figure of speech now. Blake Bravo was only fifty-eight, but he looked much older. He could have been seventy. Or even eighty.

The pale eyes narrowed as they focused on Marsh. "You came." The voice was low, a whispered rasp, like the hiss of a snake.

"Hello, Dad."

"Nice suit."

"I like it."

Blake grinned a grin to match his eyes—feral, wolfish. "Made it big after all, up there in the windy city. Didn't you?"

"I've done all right."

Blake let out a low, unpleasant chuckle. "I know

you have. I know everything about you. Don't think that I don't. I know the name of that dinky college where you managed to get yourself a four-year degree, slaving away at those books and running that company you started at the same time. I've kept track of you. I could have come after you anytime I'd wanted to. You'd be surprised the tricks your old dad has up his sleeve."

"No. I wouldn't."

The eerie eyes narrowed further and Blake's wrinkled slit of a lip curled in a sneer. "I don't like your attitude, Mr. Big Shot." He let out a ragged sigh. "But then, I never did..." He lifted that skeletal hand once more, waved it weakly and turned his face away again.

Marsh waited. He had a number of questions he might have asked. But he didn't ask them. He knew his father. A decade would not have changed the nature of the man. Blake Bravo loved it when people asked him questions. It gave him the opportunity to withhold answers.

Marsh looked beyond the wasted figure on the bed and out the room's one tall, narrow window. They were on an upper floor. All he could see was a section of gunmetal-gray sky. Oklahoma in May. Sunny one minute, storming the next, always the possibility that a cold front would slam up against a warm one and a funnel cloud would form.

But probably not today. The clouds rose up, dark and high, when tornadoes threatened. Today's sky was one even, uneventful expanse of gray.

The pale eyes were on him again. "I'm dying."

Marsh gave the smallest of nods. His father had said

that already. On the phone less than twenty-four hours ago. The surgeon Marsh had spoken with before he entered his father's room had told him that Blake's prognosis was hopeful. But looking at Blake now, Marsh decided that the doctor had either been kind—or a liar.

"Heart attack," Blake whispered in that snake-hiss voice of his. "A bad one. And another one coming on soon. I can feel it. I know it—but I told you that, didn't I?"

"Yes. On the phone."

"I'm slipping. Repeating myself."

Marsh shrugged. "It's all right."

"The hell it is."

They looked at each other, a long look, a look with challenge in it. And stubbornness—coming from both sides.

Then Blake spoke again. "It's my heart that's failing me. But my brother died of a stroke. Massive cerebral hemorrhage. It'll be thirty years ago come November. Thirty years..." The low rasp faded off. Blake sucked in a breath through the oxygen tube and went on, "He was only thirty-three, can you believe it?" He arched a gray and grizzled brow. "Freak thing, really. He'd been...how should I put it? Under a hell of a lot of stress in the months right before his...unfortunate demise."

Marsh still said nothing. What good would it do? He knew his father's sick games. Let the old man play it out by himself this time.

Blake wheezed. "Have a little trouble...getting

air.'' Then he prodded, ''Well. Don't you want to know about your uncle?''

Marsh didn't. Why should he? He doubted there even was an uncle. ''You'll say what you want to say—whatever it is I guess you got me here to say. No point in my interrupting.''

There was more chuckling. The low laughter made Blake cough. The cough had an ugly sound. It also dislodged the oxygen tube, which Blake slowly and wearily hooked back in place.

''Ugh,'' he said, when the thing was anchored in his nose again. ''Disgusting, this dying...'' He shot his son another look. ''Admit it. You never knew I had a brother, did you?''

''You're right. I didn't know you had a brother.''

''There are lots of things you don't know.''

''I'm sure you're right about that, too, Dad.''

''Damn right, I'm right.'' Blake wheezed some more. He closed his eyes.

The room was silent again. Marsh watched the clear liquid drip from the IV bag into the tube hooked to the back of his father's hand. Out in the hall he heard someone with squeaky shocs striding by.

''So damn tired,'' said the old man on the bed. ''And the meds they give me mess with my mind. And you...you're slowing me down, Mr. Big Shot. You're not asking the questions.''

Marsh almost smiled at that, though it would have been a smile completely lacking in warmth. And then he let the dying man have what he wanted. ''All right, Dad. Why did you ask me to come here?''

''I didn't ask.''

"You're right. You're always right. Why did you *demand* that I come here?"

Blake's lip curled again, in a smirk of weary amusement. "Dying's expensive. Somebody's got to pay the damn hospital bill."

"No problem. I'll cover it."

"It's nothing to you, huh? Big shot like you?"

"I said, I'll cover it." Marsh spoke with more irritation than he meant to.

"Well, well," said his father. "All got up in a pricey suit. But you're not so changed, after all. You never did like me calling you big shot. You still don't like it, do you?"

Marsh decided to ignore that question. "So that's all? You needed someone to pick up the tab."

"You wish."

"Why am I here, Dad?"

"That's the third time you've asked." The pale eyes gleamed at the petty triumph. "And I was just razzing you about the bill. I can cover it. You'll find out. I have...various hidden assets, shall we say?"

Marsh could believe that. When he was growing up, his father had never held a job that Marsh could remember. Sometimes Blake would disappear for months on end. Maybe he worked then, though he never said anything about a job. Marsh's mother was the one who worked. Tammy Rae Sandovich Bravo had labored long and hard at an endless string of dead-end jobs, in order to support her family. Marsh had assumed that his mother earned what little they had. But then she died when he was sixteen. And somehow there was still food in the rundown shack where they lived. Somehow the electric bill always got paid before OG&E cut off their service.

His father was still talking, the snake-hiss voice weighted now with self-satisfaction. ''Uh-huh. *Hidden* assets. Assets *safely* tucked away, you might say. And as my son and chosen heir, it'll all be yours when I go.''

Marsh went ahead and asked, though he knew he wouldn't get an answer. ''What'll be mine, Dad?''

''You'll find out. Soon enough. You have a big, *glittery* surprise in store, I'll tell you that much. A girl's best friend, as they say. But in this case, it's a *boy's* best friend, a *big shot's* best friend, now isn't it?''

Marsh only looked at him.

Blake grinned his death's head grin. ''You haven't got a clue, have you? And I like that. You *know* I like that. That's where the fun is. Thirty years' worth of fun—and they'll never catch me now. They'd have to track me down in hell.'' He started to laugh, but didn't have the strength for it. The laugh became little more than an exhausted, wheezing sigh. ''Damn. Tired...'' He swore, low and crudely. ''Always tired now...''

The mad eyes drooped shut—then popped opened again. ''So that's why you're here—or at least half of it. Your big surprise. Your...legacy, why don't we call it? But you can't have that till I'm gone.''

Marsh could feel his patience giving way. ''Leave it to charity, whatever it is. I don't want it.''

Blake clucked his tongue. ''Always the big shot. Never needed a damn thing from your dear old dad.... Just remember, when the time comes. Start where I never let you go. I've made it easy for you, once you start looking.''

Marsh said nothing. He didn't like what he was feeling. He'd spent ten years recreating himself. And all it took was ten minutes of conversation with his father and he was eighteen again, his hands balling into fists.

''Suck up your guts, Mr. Big Shot,'' Blake taunted. ''Hold that killer instinct in check.'' He lifted his right hand, the one free of IV lines, and raked the lank, thinning gray hair off his heavily lined forehead. Marsh saw it then: a small white starburst of scar tissue right over where the blue pulse throbbed at his father's temple.

''See that?'' the old man hissed. ''Were you wondering? Well, there it is, what you did to your dear old dad that last time.''

Marsh stared at the scar, remembering things he'd just as soon have forgotten. He breathed deeply, ordered his fists to relax, reminded himself that he was a grown man now. He'd gotten beyond all this old garbage. He didn't have to play Blake Bravo's sick cat-and-mouse games anymore.

Blake dropped his hand, so that the hair hid the scar again. But he wouldn't shut up. ''Let nature do it for you,'' he suggested in that papery whisper of his. ''It's not going to be that long.''

Marsh dragged in one more long, slow breath. The deep breaths were working, to a degree. His heart rate had slowed, his hands had relaxed.

He said in an even tone, ''Dad. It's been an experience, getting in touch again.''

Blake winked at him. “That it has, my boy—and do you think you're leaving town now?”

It would have given Marsh great satisfaction to answer, I don't *think* I'm leaving. I *am* leaving.

But he wasn't going anywhere—except to find himself a decent hotel. Evidently, Marsh still possessed some shred of filial emotion. He would stay, for a few days. He would be there if the end did come.

“No,” he said. “I'll stay in town for a day or two.”

“That's right, you will. They cut me open, cracked my chest bone like a pecan shell—did I tell you?”

“You did.”

“Three days ago, that was. Quintuple bypass. And a little plastic valve. I can hear that valve, whooshing open, swinging shut, when it's quiet, when I'm alone.... All that cutting they did, all those fancy repairs. They won't be enough. I'll be dead. And soon.”

Marsh just shook his head, even as a soft voice inside him whispered that his father was right.

“Shake your head all you want,” Blake said. “You'll see if I don't know what I'm talking about.”

“Your doctor said otherwise.”

“Doctors.” Blake let out another gutter expletive. “What the hell do they know?” The question was purely rhetorical. Without waiting for an answer, Blake switched to the next item on his personal agenda. “And now, for your *other* surprise...”

Marsh simply did not want to hear it. “I think you should rest now.”

“Rest. Hah. Fat lot of good rest'll do me.”

Marsh turned for the door.

“Where do you think you're going?”

"To find a place to stay."

"You can stay at the house."

An image of the dreary shack hidden among the oaks and hickories down a dirt road out east of town flashed through Marsh's mind. "No, thanks."

"No great love for the old homestead, huh?"

"I'll see you later, Dad."

"Wait."

Marsh shouldn't have, but he paused, his hand poised on the doorknob.

"You'll need my keys. Even having a heart attack, I had the sense to lock up what was mine." The whispery voice had pride in it now. "I called the ambulance and locked up and went out to wait on the front step. By the time they got there, I was curled up on the ground. But I locked up what was mine, you can count on that." He tipped his head in the direction of a tall cabinet near the door to the bathroom. "Keys're in my pants. In there—and you remember the rules. I know you do. You won't go nosin' around in my things till I'm gone for good, will you?"

"I said I'm not staying at the house."

"Take the damn keys, anyway. I'm never going to be using them again."

Marsh turned the steel doorknob.

"I'm not finished," his father said.

"Whatever it is, you can tell me later."

His father went on as if Marsh hadn't spoken. "That girl," he whispered. "That pretty redhead. The doctor's daughter..."

Marsh stood absolutely still, his face a mask. Whatever the mention of Tory did to him, he wouldn't give Blake Bravo the satisfaction of seeing it.

Blake was grinning again. "You call her. You remember the number, don't you? It hasn't changed."

Marsh pulled open the door. "I'll be back to check on you. Tonight, probably."

"Call her," his father commanded again. "You'll see. You're going to love it, the redhead's surprise."

Marsh gave his father no chance to say more. He stepped out into the hall, drawing the door shut in his wake.

Five minutes later, he was behind the wheel of his rental car. He left the hospital parking lot and drove south until he came to Gray. Then he turned west. Without even having to think about it, he worked his way over to Main at the point where Main became a two-way street.

Norman, Oklahoma. His hometown. It all looked... bigger. More prosperous. The streets were more crowded than he remembered. But in a basic sense, it was the same. He still recalled which way to turn to get where he wanted to go—which was toward the interstate, where he knew he'd find a large hotel.

He passed the high school, noted that they were putting a new front on it. The wooden statue still stood at Main and Wylie. Somebody's ancestor, a Union soldier in the War Between the States, carved from a tree trunk by a chainsaw artist, if Marsh remembered right.

A couple of blocks past the statue was the first street he might have turned on, if...

Marsh did *not* turn onto that street. Nor did he turn at the one after it, or the one after that, though any one of those three would have taken him quickly to the handsome brick house where his high school sweetheart—the girl he'd sworn to love forever, the girl who'd sworn the same to him—had lived.

His father's raspy whisper echoed in his brain.

Call her. You'll see. You're going to love it, the redhead's surprise….

Marsh told himself he was ignoring that whisper. There was no surprise. His father was just doing what his father always did: trying to stir up trouble wherever he sensed an opportunity.

Marsh told himself a few other things: that he would *not* call her. That he had set her free of him years ago, that she probably would only slam the door in his face if he showed up out of nowhere right now. That he'd come back to his hometown because his father was dying and for no other reason.

That bygones needed to remain bygones.

Sleeping dogs should be left to lie.

Water under the bridge must just keep flowing on its way.

That she was probably married with children by now. Married, a mother—and happy. With a good life that didn't include the bad boy she'd loved in her foolish youth. That she deserved the best and he sincerely hoped she had found it.

Still…

He had loved her with his whole heart and soul—desperately. Completely. There had been no one else in the past ten years who even came close to taking her place.

Marsh blinked.

Damn. He'd already crossed the interstate and driven right past Sooner Mall. He was well beyond the area where he could look for a place to stay. Swearing under his breath, he swung into the left lane, executed a U-turn and told himself to pay attention to the task at hand.

He found a hotel a few minutes later. It wasn't until after he'd checked in and called his office in Chicago to see how things were going there that thoughts of Tory crept into his mind again.

He ordered those thoughts away. The hotel had a small gym. He went down there and worked out for an hour. Then he spent some time sweating in the sauna. And after that, he cleaned up.

By then it was a little after six. And he was thinking of Tory again. What, he wondered, was her life like now?

Had the old man been telling the truth? Did she still live in that big brick house on that wide tree-lined street in Westwood Estates, with her parents?

Bygones and sleeping dogs, he thought.

Let her alone. She would not want to see you....

Still, he got the phone book out of his sitting-room desk drawer and turned to physicians in the yellow pages. He found no listing for a Dr. Seth Winningham. He flipped to the white pages. No Seth or Audra Winningham there, either. It could have been, of course, that they had merely decided to go *un*listed.

But then he saw it: V. J. Winningham. *V* for Victoria. *J* for Justine. Same address, same phone number. Just as the old man had said. The doctor and his wife had probably retired, moved down to Florida or out to Arizona and left the house to their only child.

And her last name was still Winningham. She hadn't married—or at least, it appeared that way. But then, you could never tell for certain by a name. Some women kept their maiden names even after they'd said, "I do."

Marsh sat for a long time with the open phone book in his lap, staring at the number he remembered so well and coming to grips with the inevitable.

He wasn't going to be able to stop himself from giving that number a try.

Chapter Two

"Tory?"

That was all the voice on the other end of the line said. Just her name. Cautiously. On a rising inflection.

Just her name.

And the sound sent Tory Winningham's world spinning into chaos.

She would know that voice anywhere. Even after ten years.

Her stomach churning, she cast a frantic glance at the table a foot away.

"Tory?" His voice in her ear again, more insistent now. "Hello? Tory?"

Kim *was* watching. And she picked up on her mother's distress. The pixie face scrunched into an apprehensive frown. "Mama. Who's that? What's the matter?"

Tory spoke into the phone. "Just a minute, please." She wrapped her hand around the receiver, so the man on the other end couldn't hear. Then she summoned every ounce of will and self-control she possessed and mustered a reassuring smile. "It is just an old friend of mine, honey. No one you know. Eat."

For a split second that felt like infinity, Kim stared at Tory, still frowning. Then her expression relaxed. She shrugged and picked up her fork again.

Turning her back to her daughter, Tory spoke to her caller. "Yes." Her windpipe clamped shut. She had to swallow to make it open, to get air. At last she managed to fill her lungs. "This is Tory."

"It's Marsh," he said. Then he added his last name, "Bravo," as if she might have—or even *could* have—forgotten.

Stay calm, girl, she thought. Don't let your voice go giving you away. "Yes. Yes, I know."

After a taut, agonizing moment, he spoke again. "This is pretty crazy, I realize. After all this time..." His deep voice was hesitant, hopeful.

"Yes." She kept thinking, Breathe. Relax. Speak calmly. Her throat felt so terribly dry. "Crazy," she said. "That's the right word for it."

"You're not..." He paused. She could hear him, doing what she kept doing. Breathing. Slowly. Deliberately. With such painful care. Finally he spoke again. "I don't know how to ask, except to just say it. Are you married?"

Why? she longed to demand. What do you care? It is too late now, Marsh Bravo. You made your choice ten years ago.

"Tory?"

"No," she said, very softly. "No, I am not..." She let her voice trail off rather than say that dangerous word: *married.*

Another silence. Behind her, Kim had just taken a gulp of milk. Tory knew this because she heard the clink of her glass as she set it back on the table.

"Is it...a bad time?" he asked, his tone suddenly hushed.

She didn't like the hesitancy of his question or the lowered tone. What did it all mean? Did he...? Was it possible that he *knew?*

"Tory, are you still there?"

She sent a swift glance over her shoulder at her daughter, who, thank the good Lord, was concentrating on her tuna casserole. "As a matter of fact," she said into the phone, "I am eating dinner now."

Yet another silence, but this time a brief one. Then he said, "Look. I know I've got no damn right to ask you. I know I told you to forget all about me. But I...Tory, I'd really like to see you. Can you meet me somewhere? For a drink, maybe?"

He does know, she thought. He must know. That's why he's called. He probably talked to his father and that awful old man has finally told him.

Tory closed her eyes—and saw Blake Bravo's face. Grinning at her, that ugly, mean grin of his. She shook her head to banish the image—and found herself wondering why, if Marsh knew, he didn't just say so.

"Listen," she said, "is there a number where I can call you back a little later tonight?"

"You mean you can't talk now." It was a statement, and a grim one.

"Yes, that is what I mean."

"Let me give you my cell phone number."

Those words caused faint hope to rise. Maybe he wasn't even in town yet. Maybe he was miles away, in another state. Maybe it was all just talk, and he would never come at all. Maybe—

But then he spoke again. He mentioned the name of a certain hotel, and an address less than two miles from her house. Her dread returned full force, making her heart thud loudly and bringing a faint taste of copper to her mouth. He said something about his father. About a heart attack.

Still painfully aware of Kimmy behind her, she gave out a bland expression of sympathy. "I am so sorry to hear that."

"Why?" he asked dryly. "I don't think anyone else is."

"Is he—"

He answered before she completed the question. "He's still alive. As of now. But it doesn't look good. They've got him over at Norman Regional."

She wanted to cry out, What did he say about me? Did he tell you? Is that it? Is that why you've called?

She asked, very carefully, "Have you...talked to him yet?"

"I saw him a couple of hours ago."

"And?"

"He's very sick. Other than that, he hasn't changed a bit. What time will you call?"

She bit the inside of her lip and accepted the fact

that if Marsh *did* know about Kimmy, he wasn't going to talk about it now.

Which was a good thing. She couldn't *afford* to talk about it now, anyway.

She glanced at the stove clock—6:23. After dinner Kim would be busy with homework. ''In an hour?''

''Good enough.''

She hung up, gave herself a few seconds to compose her features, then turned back to the table and slid into the chair across from her daughter.

Kimmy, always a good eater, had finished her casserole and her salad. She'd started in on a drop biscuit. The biscuit was giving her trouble, breaking apart as she tried to butter it.

''Here.'' Tory held out her hand—which surprised her by not shaking one bit. Kim passed the biscuit across. Tory buttered it. Kim watched the process with great interest. ''Jam?'' Tory asked.

''Um. Yes, please.''

Tory spooned a dab of strawberry jam onto each crumbly biscuit half. ''There you go.'' She set the halves back on Kim's plate.

Kim picked one up and brought it to her mouth. Before she bit into it, she asked, ''Who was that you were talking to?''

Tory's smile felt like something glued onto her face. ''Just an old friend.''

Kim set the biscuit half down again. ''You said that before. What old friend? Who?''

''No one you know.''

''You said that before, too.''

Tory faked a warning frown. "And that is all I am going to say, Miss Nosy Pants."

Kimmy groaned. "Mama. Pants can't be nosy."

"Eat that biscuit. And finish your milk."

"Then can I have a Ding-Dong?"

"The milk and the biscuit. Now."

Tory spent the next hour trying not to let her daughter see her distress, and seesawing back and forth between acceptance of the fact that she would have to meet with Marsh and frustrated fury that such a thing should be necessary.

After all this time.

After she'd accomplished what she would once have called impossible—letting go of her lovesick dream that Marsh would someday return to her, would go down on one knee and beg her to marry him, would swear he couldn't live another minute without her at his side.

It hadn't been easy, but lately Tory had managed to achieve a pleasant, peaceful kind of balance in her life. Her parents, in their forties when she was born and now both nearing seventy, had retired to New Mexico. They had left their roomy ranch-style house to Tory and their beloved granddaughter. Tory owned her own business and enjoyed her work. Her daughter was beautiful, healthy, bright and well adjusted.

Things were going great.

And now this.

Marsh Bravo—back in town.

His return could shatter everything, could turn her

peaceful life upside down—just as his leaving had done a decade before.

Still…

Marsh Bravo was her daughter's father.

That fact remained, undeniable. He had a right to know his child.

And Kim did ask about him. More and more often of late. In the end Tory really didn't have much of a choice in the matter, and she knew it. She would have to meet with him.

When Tory called Marsh back, she did it from the privacy of her bedroom, with the door closed. She'd already gotten hold of Betsy, the high school girl who lived three doors up the street. As a general rule, Tory used Betsy Tilden whenever Rayanne Pickett, next door, was unavailable.

Rayanne Pickett was like a member of Tory's family. She was a dear friend to Tory's mother and as good as an extra grandma to Kim. Tonight, though, Tory didn't want to take the chance that Rayanne might question her about where she suddenly had to get off to, after nine on a weeknight. Rayanne, like Tory's parents, would not be thrilled to learn that the boy who had gotten Tory in trouble had returned to town.

True, chances were that Rayanne would have to know eventually.

But ''eventually'' was not tonight.

So Tory had asked Betsy first. And Betsy had agreed to come over at nine-fifteen, after Kim went to bed.

Tory kept the second phone conversation with

Marsh brief. ''I'll meet you in the lobby of your hotel,'' she said after a terse exchange of greetings. ''About nine-thirty?''

He didn't try to keep her talking, only said, ''That's fine—and Tory?''

''Yes?''

''Thanks. For agreeing to see me.''

She didn't know what to say to that, so she didn't say anything, just quietly set the phone in its cradle.

Tory agonized over whether or not to tell Kim that she was going out. As long as Kim stayed in bed where she belonged, she didn't have to know. But then, if Tory said nothing, and Kim woke up and found her gone—no. That wouldn't do.

So when bedtime came, Tory told her daughter that she had to go out for a while, that Betsy would be there if Kim needed anything. Kim asked the logical question, the one Tory had been dreading.

''Where are you going?''

''It's grown-up business,'' Tory said, choosing evasion over an outright lie.

Kim got the message. ''You mean you won't tell me.''

''That's right. But I promise. I won't be gone too long.''

A crafty light came into Kimmy's big dark eyes—eyes she'd inherited from the father she'd never met. Yet. ''You know what? I think I should stay up. I can keep Betsy company and wait for you to get home.''

Tory cut that idea off at the pass. ''Uh-uh. Betsy will have homework to keep her busy. And you can wait for me just fine—right here in your comfy bed, with the lights out.''

''Aw, Mom...''

''Give me a kiss.''

''Oh, all right.''

Betsy arrived at exactly 9:15. Tory thanked the girl for coming on such short notice, invited her to help herself to anything in the refrigerator and promised to return by eleven at the very latest. Betsy waved a hand and told Tory not to think she had to rush.

Tory went out to the garage and got into her car. It was then, as she slid behind the wheel, that her heart decided to start racing and her hands began to shake.

She flipped down the visor and lifted the cover on the lighted mirror built into it. ''Calm down. Take it easy. Everything is going to be all right,'' she whispered to her own reflection.

It didn't seem to do much good. Her heart still pounded too hard and her hands kept on quivering.

She shut the mirror, flipped the visor up and started the car.

The drive was a short one. And the closer she got, the faster her heart seemed to beat. She was nothing short of a nervous wreck by the time she nosed her car into an empty space about twenty feet from the hotel's front entrance.

Was this really happening? Somehow it didn't feel real. Would she even recognize him? Would *he* recognize her? And what, if anything, did he know about Kim? What should she say if he *did* know? And what if he didn't?

Lord. It all went around and around.

And at the center of it was Kimmy.

Tory had never lied to her daughter about Marsh. Kim knew that Tory had loved Kim's father with all of her heart. Tory had explained how he had had to go away suddenly, how she had tried to get in touch with him, but never knew where he had gone and so could not find him.

The story, which *was* the truth, had been enough until just recently. But lately Kim's questions kept getting tougher.

"Don't you think we better look a little harder now?" she would ask. "Don't you think he needs to know he has me? Don't you think it's something that he would really *want* to know?"

"Yes," Tory always answered, a catch in her throat. "Of course he would want to know. And we *will* start looking. Very soon."

That kind of reply wasn't going to work for much longer.

And now, well, maybe it wouldn't have to.

That would be good.

Wouldn't it?

Tory got out of her car. The wind was up and a light, misty rain had started falling. The wind plastered her skirt to her thighs and blew her hair across her face. Absently Tory raked her hair back out of the way and made for the wall of glass that led to the hotel lobby.

The automatic doors swung wide as she reached them. Tory stepped between them, entering a vestibule. She felt windblown and a little soggy and more nervous than ever. Just keep moving, she thought. And she did, taking big, determined strides. Another set of doors swung open for her and she entered the lobby.

She saw him immediately.

He stood near the marble-topped check-in desk.

Oh, God. Her silly heart was flopping around in her chest like a landed trout.

He was different—and yet not different. The square-jawed, full-lipped, wonderful face—a face she'd always thought belonged on a poet or a priest—was the same. So was the thick brown hair, though it was cut somewhat shorter now. And those eyes—deep-set, heavily lashed. Those eyes had not changed at all.

He had filled out. He was broader in the shoulders, deeper in the chest.

No trace of boy left, she thought with a sinking feeling that might have been dismay. All man, now…

And his clothes…expensive clothes. Good slacks, a high-dollar polo shirt with a tiny designer monogram on the pocket. And his shoes…

Fine, beautifully made shoes.

Shoes that looked as if they cost a good sight more than the 150 baby-sitting dollars she had pressed into his hand on the night he left her—money he did pay back. She'd found it tucked into the only letter he sent her three months later, the one that said she should forget him, that he was no good and she could do better and he wasn't coming back, after all.

He was never coming back….

For some crazy reason, looking at him now, Tory felt the heart-stopping pain of that letter all over again. Standing in that hotel lobby, windblown and rain-damp, her gaze locked with his, she was spinning back in time.

She was sixteen again, and four months' pregnant, barely a child herself, about to have a child—a girl who had waited with longing in her heart. A girl who had trusted. A terrified girl who loved with fierce abandon, a girl who was going to have to get used to the idea that she and her unborn child would be facing the future alone.

That had been the lowest point, the worst for her—reading that letter. Worse even than that last night—the night he finally turned on his father and gave Blake Bravo a large taste of his own bitter medicine.

He had cried in her arms that night.

And there had been blood—most of it dried by then.

She remembered that so clearly, how black bloodstains can look in the moonlight.

When she sneaked out to meet him and saw the blood smeared all over him, she'd had to put her hand over her own mouth to keep from crying out.

He saw her fear for him in her eyes and shook his head. "It's not my blood—not most of it, anyway. It's *his*. My dad's blood..." With a low, anguished moan, he reached for her.

And she went into his arms, held him, though she feared that the blood would smear on her, too, that later she would have to hide that pair of pajamas in the bottom of a drawer until she could sneak them outside and bury them deep in a full trash can.

He whispered to her between ragged sobs. "I hit him. Hard. More than once. And when he finally went down, he cracked his head on the side of the table. God, Tory. I think I killed him...."

She held him tighter, stroked him with soothing hands, murmured tender lies—that it was okay, that everything would be all right.

He said, "I called the ambulance. And then I hid, in the trees, until they came. They took him out. He was so still, but maybe...he *could* have been alive. There were cops, too. They looked around the property, but they didn't find me. Tory, I have to get away. I have to get out of town...."

She begged him to stay. But he said he couldn't. He'd end up in jail if he stayed. So she said she would go with him.

"You can't. You're sixteen. How would we live? It would never work. But I'll come back, Tory. I swear. Someday..."

Someday.

She hadn't liked the sound of that at all. Someday could be forever. Someday could mean *years*.

But what could she do? She sneaked back into the house to get what money she had there, and then came out again and gave it to him. And after he left, in the house once more, she tiptoed to the hall bathroom, locked the door and turned on the light, expecting to find dark stains all over herself.

There was nothing. Her eyes looked wide and haunted in the big bathroom mirror, but her blue pajamas bore not a single dark smear. The blood had all dried on him before he came to her.

Before he left he had asked her to find out what she

could about Blake. He promised to call. In a few days…

And he *had* called. Once. Three days after that terrible night. He called in the late afternoon, when her father was still at his clinic and her mother was at the beauty shop.

By then Tory had thought that everything would be all right. Because Marsh's father had not died. Blake was out of the hospital and back on his feet. She told Marsh the news, bursting with joy that it would all work out, after all.

"You can come home now, Marsh. Your father didn't die, and it's safe to come back."

"No, Tory. I can never go back there. He'll kill me if I do. And if he doesn't kill me, *I'll* kill *him*…."

He'd sounded so very far away. And so desperate. A fugitive from justice. He'd actually called himself that. He wouldn't tell her where he was calling from. He said he had to keep moving, he couldn't let Blake find him.

"You don't know him, Tory. You don't know how he is. Nobody gets the better of him…."

She was crying when she hung up the phone, thinking she'd go crazy waiting for Marsh to call again.

But she hadn't gone crazy, though sometimes in the weeks to come it had felt like she was. And as it turned out, he never did call again. That was the last time she ever spoke to him—until a few hours ago, when she'd picked up the phone and heard his voice saying her name.

A dark-haired woman wearing too much perfume

brushed past her murmuring, "Excuse me," as she went.

"Oh." Tory blinked. "It's okay..."

A black leather wing chair waited a few feet from where Tory stood. She ordered her numb legs to move, to take her there. Once she reached it, she sank stiffly into it.

Marsh came toward her. So strange. Her heart was breaking all over again. It shouldn't be like this, shouldn't *feel* like this, not after all these years.

He stopped just a foot from her chair. Concern had turned those dark eyes to velvet. "God. Tory..."

Almost, she lifted up her arms to him.

Almost, she surged from that chair and into his embrace.

Almost.

But not quite.

She hesitated, thought, Do I really want that—his arms around me? And how can I be certain that he will welcome me there?

Then she realized it didn't matter whether she wanted him to hold her, whether he wanted her body pressed close to his. Somehow, while she hovered on the brink of throwing herself at him, the dangerous moment had passed.

Tory stayed in the chair and stared up at him. "Why now?" The hushed words seemed to come out all on their own. "Why now, after all this time?"

"Tory, I—" He cut off his answer before he even said it. "Please. I think we'd better go somewhere more private. To my room, all right?"

She probably should have said no to that. But she

didn't. People kept strolling by them, and there were three clerks behind the check-in desk. She didn't need any of those people witnessing her distress, let alone hearing whatever she and this man ended up saying to each other.

She stood on shaky legs and smoothed her rumpled skirt. "All right."

For a moment she thought he would take her arm. She didn't know if she could bear that—his touch, right then.

But then he only gestured. "This way."

She fell in step beside him. They strolled across the lobby and down into a central court area paved in stone. Then up three carpeted steps to the elevators. He pushed a button. They waited. She didn't look at him. It seemed better not to.

A set of doors opened. They got on with two men in business suits. The elevator had glass walls. They rode up with a view of the open court area retreating below them.

The two businessmen were arguing, speaking in tight, hushed tones. Tory ignored them. It wasn't hard. Most of her energy was taken up in painful awareness of the man beside her—the man she still would not look at. She stared blindly down at the courtyard as it moved away beneath them.

The businessmen got off on the fourth floor, leaving Tory and Marsh alone the rest of the way. Marsh didn't speak. And Tory felt that she *couldn't* speak, that if she'd opened her mouth only a strangled, crazy moan would come out.

At last, they reached his floor—the top floor. The car stopped, the doors slid open.

He said, ''This way,'' for the second time. She walked beside him, down a hall that was also a long balcony overlooking the courtyard below. When they reached his door, she stepped back as he used his key card. The green light blinked. He turned the handle and signaled for her to go in ahead of him.

It was a suite, she noted with some relief. She wouldn't have to try to talk to him in a room that was more than 50 percent bed.

They entered a small entrance hall that opened onto a living area done in forest-green and maroon. Soothing colors, she thought, though the last thing she felt at that moment was soothed.

He gestured at the forest-green sofa. Obediently she lowered herself onto one end of it.

''Can I get you a drink?''

Her stomach rebelled at the thought. Yet she heard herself answer, ''Plain tonic water?''

''I can do that.''

He turned for the bar, which had a mirrored wall behind it, and got busy fixing the drink she'd asked for that she really didn't want. Once he'd poured the tonic water, she watched him mix himself a whisky and soda.

She couldn't help staring at his hands. Very fine hands, long-fingered and strong. They appeared much better cared for than in the past, the nails filed short and buffed smooth.

She found herself thinking how they used to hold hands all the time, thinking that she could still recall exactly the way his hand had felt in hers—warm and firm and rough.

And then she thought what she should not have allowed herself to think.

But holding hands wasn't what got us into trouble…

What got them into trouble had happened out by the river at Ten Mile Flat, in the back seat of that old Plymouth Duster he used to drive. They would lie all wrapped up together, clothes unbuttoned, but never fully undressed—after all, someone *might* come along. Surprising, the trouble a couple of kids can get into, and all without ever taking off all their clothes.

As if he were touching her now, she could feel them—those long hands on her skin…

Tory blinked. Gulped. Cut her eyes away.

When she looked back, he was watching her in the mirror over the bar. She became certain, in that instant, that he could see inside her mind, that he knew what she had been thinking, about those nights out at Ten Mile Flat.

She felt defiant, then. And angry. That she should still remember so vividly. That this man who had left her to have his baby alone could still call forth such a powerful response in her.

He turned, a glass in each hand, and came to sit in the armchair nearest her end of the sofa. He passed her the tonic water. The glass was cold, beads of moisture already sliding down the sides. She took one sip. Her stomach lurched.

No. Better not try to finish it. She set it on the coffee

table in front of her. He drank, the ice cubes clinking together in his glass.

She found herself staring at his watch. A Rolex. Unbelievable.

She said what she was thinking. "It looks like you are doing well."

He lifted one of those broad shoulders in a half shrug. "I own a business. Boulevard Limousine of Chicago. I started it eight years ago, with one twelve-year-old Cadillac limousine and one chauffeur—me. Originally, it was just a way to support myself while I was earning my degree."

His degree? Marsh Bravo, who had barely managed to graduate from Norman High, now had a college degree?

He chuckled. "Hard to believe, huh? Me, a college graduate. But I have to confess. It's not from any college you would have heard of. You went to OU, I suppose."

"Yes. I did."

"Figured you would. Dean's honor list, right?"

She nodded. "And...how is your business doing now?"

He brought his glass to that sensual mouth again, sipped, shrugged once more. "Revenues this year should top five million. I have 250 employees and a fleet of 85 limousines."

Tory could hardly believe what she was hearing.

I'm no good, he had written. *You can do better....*

Eight years ago, he'd said. Eight years ago, in Chicago, he had started his business. And since then, he must have been making a living at least, must have been doing all right.

Yet he had never called. Never written. Never made the slightest effort to see her, until now.

That hurt. That hurt way too much.

She couldn't afford that—to start hurting for this man all over again. Couldn't. And *wouldn't.*

She had to remember. This meeting was not about her. It was about Kim. *For* Kim. Kim was the one who mattered now. And if Kim's long-lost daddy owned a fleet of limousines, well, that was all to the good.

Marsh looked into his glass, and then back up at Tory. "What about you?"

She stared at him blankly, still trying to accept the fact that the poor boy she had so passionately, utterly loved, the poor boy who had turned his back on her because he had nothing to offer her, had spent the past decade becoming a rich man.

At last, his question registered. He wanted to know what she did for a living. "I'm a florist. I have my own shop. The Posy Peddler. On Gray."

"A florist." He smiled.

Did he find florists amusing? She pulled her shoulders back. "That's right."

He gave her a long, nerve-racking look. Then he spoke gently. "You said on the phone that you weren't married. Is there...someone special, then?"

Someone special? Why did he ask that? What difference could it make to him, now, after all this time?

It was too much. She stood, then didn't know what to do next. She started to sit again, but changed her mind about that. She stayed upright, and wrapped her arms around her stomach, which felt as if someone had tied it into a ball of hard knots. "I don't— Marsh. Why are you here? Why now?"

Marsh looked up at her, wondering what he'd said that had made her so angry all of a sudden, recalling how crushed she had looked at the sight of him down in the lobby, how he'd wanted to grab her and hold her close and plead with her to forgive him for not coming back—to swear to protect her, to never hurt her again.

But he hadn't grabbed her. And she hadn't thrown herself into his arms.

And since then, things seemed to have gone seriously south. This pretty stranger glaring at him now was not the same innocent girl he had once loved so much. Once, when he looked at her, he could feel his whole heart opening up, reaching out to her.

He didn't feel that way now. He felt interest. She was a good-looking woman. And he liked the way she carried herself, liked the sound of her voice, the cute smattering of freckles across her slim nose.

It was…attraction. Yes. That was the word for it. But he didn't think it was love. Not anymore.

Could it grow into love again?

As if he would ever find out the answer. The woman glaring down at him now didn't look especially eager to try again.

But then, what had he expected? He was, after all, the one who broke it off, even if he *had* done it for her own good, even if he had known, deep down, that it could never have worked out for them.

And probably even more damning in her eyes than his breaking it off, were those letters she had sent him. The ones that had taken months to reach him, he'd moved around so much there in that first year. The letters he'd returned unopened, though it nearly killed him to do it. He'd spent a lot of nights wondering what she might have written in those letters.

"Why are you here?" she demanded again, openly angry now.

"I told you. My father—"

"Oh, you stop that. I'm not talking about your father right now and you know it. I want to know why you called *me*."

"I just..." Damn. He wasn't even sure he knew the answer to that himself. Curiosity, maybe. About what had happened to the girl he left behind. Curiosity—and a kind of longing. A longing not so much for the girl he had loved as for the heat and tenderness he'd known with her. A longing that had faded over the years, but that had never completely left him.

And then there had been the old man. Prodding. Taunting him to look Tory up.

"You just *what?*" she demanded.

"I wanted to see if—"

"Look," she said, cutting him off, apparently deciding she didn't want to hear what he had to say, after all. "This is a...well, it's a shock for me." Those beautiful blue eyes had taken on a panicked gleam. "I don't seem to be handling it real well. I didn't know...I didn't expect—"

She looked pale again, as she had in the lobby.

Worse than she had in the lobby—as if she might be sick.

Sick at the sight of him.

Hell. He deserved the Biggest Heel on the Planet Award, to have hurt her all over again this way.

It had been a stupid idea, to call her. He should have had sense enough to consider the source when the old man started in on him about her. Even on his deathbed, Blake Bravo wouldn't give up his petty mind games.

And now, for your other *surprise…*

Right.

The surprise wasn't much of a surprise, after all. Tory couldn't forgive him and wanted nothing to do with him.

Big news.

"I don't…I'm sorry," Tory stammered, her stomach still churning, all her senses on overload.

She kept thinking, *He doesn't know. But he is Kimmy's father. And she* wants *to know him. And he has a* right *to know her. I will have to tell him, somehow….*

But it was all just too much, right then. Seeing him. Remembering things that were better forgotten.

She couldn't do it. Not tonight.

She needed…a little time. To pull herself together, to get her stunned mind around the fact that he really had come back.

"I don't…I'm sorry." She sucked in a breath, swallowed. "I have to go now. Later, I can…"

He was watching her as if she was mentally deranged—and maybe she was at that moment. She sure did feel like it, like a woman who had gone clean out of her mind.

She edged out from behind the coffee table, between his chair and the sofa. "I'll talk to you later..." She was already halfway to the door. He stood, took a couple of steps toward her. She flung out a hand in a warding-off gesture. "I'll call you. I will. Tomorrow, all right?"

She fled—there was no other word for it—leaving Marsh staring at the door she had shut in his face.

Chapter Three

Marsh's instinctive reaction was to follow her.

But he held instinct in check. She clearly wanted out of that room—and away from him.

Who was he to try to hold her there?

He went back to the bar and poured himself another drink—a double that time. He sipped it slowly, thinking that he should probably get over to the hospital. He should check on his father one more time tonight, as he'd planned to do.

But no. He felt a little too edgy for a visit with the old man right now. What had just happened had been too unsettling.

Tory had acted so strangely.

If she hadn't wanted to see him, couldn't she have just said so, on the phone, right up front?

Why even agree to meet him? Why come up to his

room with him? Why put herself through that? It didn't make any damn sense.

Marsh shook his head, sipped from his drink, decided that the remark about calling him tomorrow must have been something she'd said without thinking, without meaning it. She wouldn't be calling him. He'd never hear from her again.

Which was probably for the best.

He certainly wouldn't be idiot enough to try calling *her* again.

The past truly was another country, one he had no business trying to revisit. They were two different people now, with nothing to connect them except memories that were better left to fade, finally, into nothing.

Marsh finished his drink. Then he called the hospital. He spoke to the night nurse assigned to his father's care. Blake Bravo was sleeping peacefully, the nurse said.

"If he asks, tell him I'll see him tomorrow."

The nurse said she'd be happy to pass on his message.

The misty drizzle had stopped by the time Tory got home. Betsy said she had checked on Kim fifteen minutes ago and Kim was sound asleep.

Tory paid Betsy and walked with her out the front door. The night air was moist and warm and the wind had died down. Tory stood on her front walk, watching Betsy stroll away up the street. The girl turned and gave Tory a carefree wave before she disappeared into her own house.

Betsy was fifteen. The same age Tory had been when Marsh first asked her out...

Tory shook her head. Better not get started down memory lane again. She turned and went back up the curving walk to the house. Inside, she locked up and turned off the lights.

She looked in on Kim before she went to her own room, creeping in and then waiting in the dark by Kim's bed, until her eyes adjusted. Kim lay on her side, facing the wall, the yellow comforter she had chosen herself, when the two of them redecorated her room just last fall, pulled up close around her chin.

Mother love welled up in Tory. So sweet. And yet painful, too. A child grew so fast. Nine years took forever—and went by in an instant.

When Tory's parents had learned that their daughter was going to have a baby, they had first tried to convince her to give the baby up. Tory had refused. And eventually her parents accepted the inevitable. In the end Audra and Seth Winningham had been honestly supportive, helping to take care of Kimmy in the first years, so that Tory could finish high school and even earn a business degree at OU.

And Norman, after all, was the third largest city in Oklahoma, a progressive university town with a population nearing ninety thousand now. Tory's single-mom status may have been looked at askance by the people in her nice upper-middle class neighborhood at first. But over time she had found acceptance.

It had been rough, yes, in the beginning, being a mom at seventeen. All her high school friends felt sorry for her. They were out, running around, having fun. And she was home with a baby, longing, hungering, *praying* for Marsh to come back to her.

Kimmy stirred, sighing, pushing down the covers and flopping one arm out behind her. Tory resisted the urge to cover her again. The room wasn't cold. And covering her might wake her.

Quietly Tory turned and tiptoed out.

Tomorrow, she thought, as she crossed the hall to her own room. I will call Marsh tomorrow, in the evening. I'll make arrangements to meet with him again. And I'll do a better job of it this time. This time I won't run out without telling him what both he and Kimmy need for him to know.

"You get together with the redhead?"

Blake was sitting up in bed, looking considerably better than he had the afternoon before. The oxygen tube was gone from his nose. Though the old man still wheezed with each breath, Marsh was beginning to think that maybe the heart surgeon had been right. Blake Bravo wasn't quite ready for the grave, after all.

"Well, Mr. Big Shot? Did you see her or not?"

"Feeling better, huh, Dad?"

"You're not going to answer me, are you?"

"No. I'm not."

"You didn't see her."

Marsh said nothing.

"Wait a minute," Blake wheezed. "I get it. You saw her. But she held out on you. You didn't get your surprise."

"Dad."

"What?"

"Either drop it or explain yourself."

"Where the hell's the fun in that? I'll give you a hint—no. On second thought, I won't. Go see her again."

To keep himself from saying something he would later regret, Marsh stepped over to the window and looked out. Today the sky was a broad expanse of clear blue, dotted here and there with small, cotton-like clouds. Spread out below was a parking lot. And near the building, attractive landscaping: nandinas, a redbud tree, flower beds mulched with cedar chips.

He waited, looking out, observing the progress of a big black Buick as it rolled between the rows of parked cars and finally nosed into an empty space. A man got out and strode toward the building.

Marsh turned to his father again. "You *are* feeling better, aren't you?"

Blake grunted. "Doctor said this morning that they'll be sending me home soon—as long as I make sure there's someone there to look after me."

"I'll see about hiring you a live-in nurse."

"Forget that. I don't want any stranger in my house."

Marsh looked at his father levelly. "Don't get any ideas about me taking care of you. It wouldn't work."

Blake closed his eyes, wheezed a sigh. "Don't worry. I know it. You and I wouldn't last twenty-four hours under the same roof." He looked at Marsh again, pale eyes stranger than ever—far away. And far too knowing. "Doesn't matter. Let it go. We'll see how right that doctor is...."

Marsh shook his head. "You do feel better. You look better."

"I don't want a damn funeral, you hear what I say? Who the hell would come to my funeral anyway? I want cremation, and I want you to dump my ashes in Lake Thunderbird. Got that?"

"You're not going to die now, Dad. Your doctor said so."

"What the hell does a doctor know? What do *you* know? You're dense as a post, you know that, Mr. Big Shot? You haven't even figured out the secret that little redhead's keeping from you."

Marsh turned back to the window.

"Go see her again," Blake commanded.

Marsh studied the redbud tree below. He'd always liked redbuds, liked the twisted forms the trunks could take and the pretty heart shape of the leaves.

Marsh stayed in his father's room for another hour. It was a true test of self-control, and Marsh was pleased to find himself passing it. His father jeered and goaded, and Marsh looked out the window. Somehow the time went by.

Finally Blake dropped off to sleep again. Marsh sat in the chair in the corner and watched him for a while, listened to the labored, watery sound of his breathing, wondered what he was going to do about home care now that it looked as if Blake was going to cheat the devil, after all—at least for a while.

Marsh also wondered at himself. That he had come here, in the first place. That he found he felt accountable for the care of a hardhearted SOB who had made his childhood a living hell and driven his mother to an early grave. Evidently, some bonds were nigh on impossible to completely sever. A man felt a responsibility to a parent, period, even if that parent had always been a damn poor excuse for a human being.

When he got tired of sitting, Marsh left the hospital room. He hung around in the waiting area for a while, got out his cell phone and called Chicago.

He spoke with his second in command at Boulevard Limousine. Nothing going on there, other than the usual—drivers who didn't report in when they were supposed to, one breakdown on a trip in from O'Hare. But somehow they always found another driver to cover, and breakdowns, with the fleet of top-quality new vehicles he owned now, were few and far between. This most recent one had caused a delay, but only a short one. They'd immediately dispatched a replacement vehicle, and the problem car had been towed to the shop.

It occurred to him that he wasn't really even needed anymore at the company he had created. He'd put together a system that worked and now it could pretty much run without him. Soon it would be time to focus his energy on expanding. Or maybe to get into something else altogether.

He went back to Blake's room, where lunch was being served. He sat in the chair and watched his father pick at his meal, tuning out the gibes and taunts, pleased to find that he was getting pretty good at not listening to things he didn't need to hear.

As a child and a badly troubled teenager, he used to practice tuning out the old man. He never got a chance to get very good at it back then, though. At that time Blake hadn't been confined to a bed. And if Marsh tried not listening to his harangues, Blake had no compunction about using whatever was handy—his fists, his belt, a baseball bat—to get his rebellious son's undivided attention.

By one Marsh was ready for lunch himself. He considered giving the cafeteria a try, but then decided he'd just as soon get out of the hospital for a while. He drove down Porter, crossing Gray and Main and continuing on toward the university. He found a certain landmark restaurant he remembered, a place that was a little dark inside, but really nice out on the patio under the clusters of red-white-and-blue Cinzano umbrellas.

The lunch rush seemed to be winding down, so he didn't have much difficulty getting a table to himself. The waitress settled him beneath an umbrella with an iced tea, a basket of chips and a menu. He crunched on the chips and considered his choices, thinking that later in the afternoon he'd start looking for that live-in nurse his father would be needing.

He glanced up from the menu to signal the waitress—and saw that he was being watched. By some character a few tables away, a guy with a broad, ruddy face and a salesman's smile.

The character squinted. "Marsh? Marsh *Bravo?*"

Suddenly the face was familiar. Take away forty pounds and add long hair and—"Bob Avery."

Bob nodded at the three other men at his table. "Be right back." He got up and strode toward Marsh. "I don't believe it."

Marsh stood. "It's been a long time." They shook hands. "You're looking good."

Bob laughed. "I'm lookin' fat. But you. Hey. Doing all right, huh?"

"Getting by."

"What did you get into?"

Marsh told him. "What about you?"

"What do you think? Insurance."

"Like your dad."

"That's right. I went in with him. Got my name on the door, two assistants and four clerks. He'll be retiring in a few years, then I'll be on my own."

"Sounds good."

"It's a living—and I married Steffie." Marsh remembered. Bob and Stefanie Sommers had been an item Marsh's senior year.

Marsh asked the next logical question. "Kids?"

"Two. A boy and a girl."

"What do you know? A lot can happen in ten years."

"Ain't that the truth." Bob was looking at him a little oddly now, it seemed to Marsh. "So," he said, and coughed into his hand. "You married?"

"No. Still single."

"Well. Ah. Have you stopped in to see Tory?" Something wasn't right, something in Bob's expression, in the hesitant, probing sound of his voice.

Marsh said in a flat tone, "I saw her briefly, last night."

Bob's rather small eyes got larger and his face got redder. "You did. Well. Great. That's, uh, some little girl you got there."

Marsh frowned. What was Bob getting at? Tory was far from little, and Marsh didn't "have" her. Bob's remark made no sense. "What was that?"

Bob gulped. Marsh watched his Adam's apple bounce up and then slide down. He glanced at his watch. "Wow. Look at the time. Gotta go. It has been great seein' you again. You take care of yourself, now."

"Sure," said Marsh, still wondering what the hell was going on. "You, too. My best to Steffie."

Bob hurried back to his own table, but only paused there long enough to grab his check and announce, a little too loudly, that he had to get back to the office.

Marsh sank to his chair again. The waitress came by. He ordered and he ate. He was back at the hospital by a little after two, stopping in at the nurses' desk to ask for a few referrals for home care. Then he went to his father's room.

Blake started right in on him, razzing him about Tory, about the damn "surprise" she was supposedly keeping from him. And now, after the way Bob Avery had behaved, Marsh was beginning to wonder if there could be more to this thing about Tory than a mean old man's crazy head games.

"You go on," said Blake for about the fifteenth time that day. "Talk to her again. And this time don't let her get away from you until she tells you the damn truth."

About then, Marsh could easily have grabbed the old man around his scrawny throat and squeezed until the wolfish eyes popped right out of their sockets, until

Blake gave in and blurted out the big secret, whatever the hell the big secret was.

But somehow he restrained himself. Mostly because he knew that strangling his father would get him nowhere. Blake would die with that ugly knowing grin on his wrinkled face.

Marsh said, "You know, Dad. You're right. I'm going to see her. Now."

"You be sure to tell her I said hi."

He drove to her flower shop, figuring she'd have to be there at that time of day. It wasn't difficult at all to find. He thought it looked charming, the windows sparkling clean, the displays attractive and eye catching. He almost parked and went in.

But he didn't. By then he'd had a little time to reconsider, time to think some more about the way she'd run out on him last night. After that, he doubted she'd be too thrilled to see him if he dared to drop in on her at her workplace.

Better to wait, now he thought about it. Wait until she closed the shop for the day. Call her at home, as he'd done last night.

How early could he call and reach her?

Well, how late did the shop stay open? He could see the hours printed on the door. But he couldn't quite make them out from the street. And he didn't dare get any closer. She might look out and see him.

Hell. This was ridiculous. He felt like a damn stalker—probably because he was behaving like one.

He drove on by the shop, turned left at the next intersection and then right on Main. Before long he was passing the statue of the Union soldier again. And this time, when he got to the street that would take him by Tory's house, he swung the wheel to the right and turned into her neighborhood.

The streets near her house looked much the same as they had ten years ago: solid, comfortable homes, mostly of brick, lots of oaks and sweet gum trees and twisted evergreen yaupon hollies. Some of the mailboxes were out at the street, clematis vines thick with star-shaped purple flowers twining over them.

There were children, a number of them, strolling along on either side of the street, wearing backpacks and swinging lunch boxes, probably just getting out of the elementary school a few blocks away. They looked happy, those kids. Contented with the world and with their place in it. No doubt they had the kind of life he'd always envied when he was growing up. They were going home to the nice brick houses, where they'd do their homework, have their friends over, sit down to dinner at six—dinner cooked by a trim, pretty mom who smiled a lot and didn't have to work her fingers to the bone just to make it from one day to the next.

He spotted it: Tory's house. A block and a half ahead, on the corner, with that big sweep of lawn front and side. He used to cut that lawn, and the lawn of the house next door to it—Mrs. Pickett's house—during those summers he worked for that gardening service. He'd cut a lot of lawns in this neighborhood, in those two summers, his sixteenth and seventeenth year.

He remembered he'd been running a lawnmower on

Tory's lawn the first time he ever laid eyes on her. She'd come out of the front door—fourteen, she must have been then, wearing shorts that showed off her pretty legs, that red hair pulled back with one of those scrunchy things. He'd almost run that mower right into the big oak in the corner of the lot.

That fall, he'd spotted her at school for the first time: a freshman. It had taken him until the following summer before he could drum up the nerve to ask her out.

Marsh drove very slowly—too slowly, probably. In this kind of neighborhood, where people kept their cars in their roomy garages and no one had the bad taste to hang out on the street, a lone man cruising a little too slowly could easily cause suspicion.

Again he felt slightly reprehensible, an intruder in the life of a woman he no longer really knew. Still, he didn't speed up as he approached. He slowed even further, taking in all the details, noting small changes. Flowers grew close to the house now, instead of low juniper bushes in a bed of white river rock. And the big door with the beveled glass in the top of it, once white, had been painted a deep green.

A group of children—four girls dressed in jeans and bright-colored T-shirts—were passing Tory's front walk just as Marsh turned her corner to drive by the front of the house. One of them, slim and dark-haired, wearing bright purple tennis shoes with thick white soles, waved at the others and started up the walk.

Marsh's mouth went dry.

He slammed his foot on the brake, stopped the car, right there, in the middle of the street, not caring in the least that the other three girls had turned to stare at him. He had eyes only for the slim one in the purple tennis shoes—the one who strolled straight up the walk to the dark-green door and let herself inside.

Chapter Four

Don't jump to conclusions, Marsh warned himself as he focused his eyes on the street ahead of him again and took his foot off the brake. All you saw was a dark-haired girl going into Tory's house.

A dark-haired girl who looked about nine or ten, damn it. Just the age the kid would be now if…

Gripping the steering wheel in a stranglehold, Marsh reached the end of Tory's street. He turned left, left again and left once more, circling her block, remembering his father's taunts, Tory's strange behavior last night, the frantic look in her eyes, the way she had practically run from his room.

And that remark of Bob Avery's—*That's some little girl you got there*—after which good old Bob suddenly couldn't backpedal out of that restaurant patio fast enough.

Marsh discovered that he understood how Tory must have felt last night. Right now he was pretty sure he felt the same way. Slightly sick, his stomach in knots. And he realized he didn't give a damn if some nosy busybody called the Norman police on him. He pulled over to the curb, parallel with Tory's side fence and stopped the car.

Was it possible?

Could Tory have had his baby?

Could he have had a daughter for—what—a little over nine years now, and not had a clue?

Dense as a post, the old man had called him today—the old man who had apparently known where to find Marsh for some time now, yet had never come after him, had never tried to exact the necessary revenge for the way his only son had finally dared to turn on him.

Or so Marsh had thought.

But what better revenge could there be than to deny a man knowledge of his own child?

He thought of those letters.

Those letters he'd sent back to Tory unopened.

Was that what he missed by not reading them: the news that he was going to be a father?

The knot in his gut yanked tighter. God. Tory. It must have been tough for her. At least at first. No wonder she couldn't forgive him for leaving her.

But then again, it had been *years*. And aside from those letters, it seemed pretty obvious she hadn't knocked herself out trying to find him. After the first couple of years, after he'd started to build his business, to get some sense of himself as the man he meant to become, he'd stopped hiding from the chance that the old man would find him. He'd lived his life in the open. And from that time on, she just might have managed to track him down—if she'd wanted to.

Anger. He felt it rising, felt it pounding in each beat of his heart. She could have found him. If she'd *wanted* to find him.

He muttered a curse—and told himself to relax. To take it easy. Not to overreact. He *had* been the one who called it off.

And until he confronted Tory and got the truth from her, he still couldn't be sure that the dark-haired child was his. She might be a neighbor's girl, or the daughter of a friend. She could even be Tory's, by some other guy….

No.

He couldn't believe that. She would have had to hook up with that guy too soon after Marsh had left town. She wouldn't have done that. She had loved him too much….

Marsh shook his head.

She had loved him too much.

Was that simple truth—or male ego talking?

Damn hard to say.

So just cool it, he told himself. Chill. Settle down.

But there was no damn way he would leave this nice, well-to-do neighborhood now. No way he was waiting until later to call.

He started the car again, nosed away from the curb and turned left at the corner. He parked right in front of the house. Then he got out of the car and strode up that sloping front walk.

* * *

Tory stood at the closed door to the hall bathroom. "Kimmy?"

"Please. I'm going to the *bathroom.*"

"Well, speed it up. We have to get back to the shop. I told Lisa I would only be gone half an hour, tops." Lisa was one of Tory's two clerk/floral designers.

"Mama. Can I *please* have a little privacy?"

"Get a move on."

"I'm *trying.*"

Right then the doorbell rang.

Kim yelled, "If that's Alicia, tell her—"

"Just finish your business, young lady—and don't forget to wash your hands." Tory headed for the front door to the sound of the toilet flushing behind her.

She came around the corner to the entryway—and saw Marsh's face through the glass in the top of her front door.

Oh, God.

She'd had it all planned for that evening. She would call him and ask to meet with him. And then, very gently, she would break the news about Kim. They would discuss how best to tell a nine-year-old girl that her father had returned to town; they'd arrange for that all-important first meeting.

But it was too late for arrangements now. She could see it in those dark eyes, which were way too much like Kimmy's eyes. Someone—probably that heartless daddy of his—had finally told him the truth.

He knew. And he looked stricken.

She forced her legs to carry her to the door. She

grasped the knob and pulled it wide. The big glass storm door remained between them. *He* opened that.

She stepped back. He came over the threshold, into her house, the storm door pulling shut on its own behind him.

She saw hurt in his eyes. And confusion. And anger, held carefully in check.

He spoke low. "I was just in the neighborhood. I..." His voice, already hollow sounding, broke. He paused, swallowed and went on, "I saw her, Tory. The little girl with the dark hair and the purple tennis shoes. Tory. Is she mine?"

Tory gave him his answer the only way she could manage right then: she nodded.

And Kim came racing down the hall. "Mom!"

Tory turned, moving instinctively to block her daughter's view of the man at the door. She forced a bright tone. "Sweetie, get your things together. You know we have to get to the shop."

Kim craned to see around her, to get a better look at the stranger at the door. "Who's that?"

Tory spoke more sternly. "Kimberly Winningham. You heard what I said. Get ready."

"But—"

"No buts. Go."

Kim started to obey—then hesitated. She fluttered the eyelashes that were every bit as long as Marsh's. "These jeans are too hot. Can I wear shorts—and my new sandals?"

"Kim—"

"Please."

"All right. Just go now. Get ready."

Kim spun away and vanished down the hall. Tory once again turned to face the man who waited, stunned and silent, at the door.

She spoke with great care. "I'm sorry. I have done this so badly. Please. Will you just...wait until tonight? We'll talk. We'll work this out. I promise you."

He stared straight at her. But at the same time, he seemed to be looking through her, his eyes dazed and far away. He muttered, "Kimberly. Kim. Her name is Kim."

"Yes." He looked so...hungry, right then. She had to give him something. "Kimberly Marsha," she said.

He blinked. "Marsha? Her middle name is—"

"Yes. For you. And right now, you have to—"

He was shaking his head. "But Tory. *Winningham?* Why not Bravo? Why didn't you give her my last—"

"Marsh. We cannot talk about this right now."

"Is my name on her birth certificate?"

"Marsh."

"Answer me."

"Yes. Yes. Your name is on it."

"Damn. I just can't believe that you—that I—"

"I mean it, Marsh. She'll be back any minute. We need some time to talk it over before we tell her. Please. You have to go."

He blinked again, then peered at her narrowly, as if her words weren't getting through to him at all. "Go?"

"Yes, Marsh. Please."

"Later. You want to tell her later."

"Yes."

"When?"

"Soon. But first, we have to talk. Seven-thirty? Your hotel."

For what seemed to Tory about half a lifetime, he said nothing. And then, at last, he nodded. "Seven-thirty. All right. Just come straight to my room."

"I'll be there."

"Swear it."

"Marsh. I *will* come."

He looked at her long and hard. Then, at last, he muttered, "All right," again. And then he just stood there, as if he had no idea what to do with himself next.

"Marsh. Please..."

He seemed to shake himself. "Yes. I know. I'm going."

He turned stiffly, like a man in a trance, pushed the storm door open again and went through it. Tory shut the inner door and then sagged against it, pressing her forehead to the beveled glass, watching as Marsh went down the walk to his car.

"Mama. What is going on?"

Dread forming what felt like a cold, hard ball of ice in her stomach, Tory turned.

Kim stood, small fists planted on skinny hips, at the entrance to the main hall. She was wearing purple shorts, a lavender T-shirt and the new sandals with the bright plastic flowers adorning the straps. There was a very determined set to her strong little jaw.

"Who was that man? What were you whispering to him about?"

Tory had no idea how to answer her daughter. She

looked away, glancing out through the glass again. Marsh was just getting into his car.

"Mom. You are scaring me."

For Tory it was a truly awful moment, one of the worst. She faced her daughter again.

Lord, what to do?

She didn't want to lie to Kim, but she wished with all her heart that she had taken some time to prepare her daughter for this—though how, exactly, she could have prepared Kim, she hadn't the slightest idea. Her mind, at that moment, felt empty, numb, incapable of rational thought.

Faintly, from outside on the street, she heard Marsh's car start up.

"Mama?" Kimmy's expression had begun to crumple. "What's the *matter* with you?"

The distress on Kim's face did the trick, banishing the ugly moment of indecision as if it had never been. Tory went to her daughter, put her hands on the small shoulders and knelt to bring the two of them eye to eye.

The words came out. Simple. Direct. Right to the point.

"That man is Marsh Bravo."

"Marsh Bravo?" Kimmy caught her lower lip between her small white teeth. Her eyes were wide—wide and dark as the bottom of a deep, deep well. "Marsh Bravo is my daddy's name."

"Yes. That's right."

"That man is—"

"Yes."

"—my daddy?" Kim spoke in awe. In wonder. In growing hope.

Tory felt the tears pushing at the back of her throat. She swallowed them down. This was not about her feelings, not about her pain.

Kimmy said, so softly, "My daddy came back?"

"Yes, honey. He did."

The small shoulders stiffened under Tory's hands. Before Tory could stop her, Kim jerked away and flew to the door. She grabbed the knob, hauled the door wide, stared in outrage at the emptiness beyond.

"He's gone! He didn't even talk to me!" She shoved on the storm door and ran out to the walk, the slick soles of her new sandals slapping hard with each step.

Tory bestirred herself, rising to her feet and following her daughter outside.

Kim looked up and then down the street, but Marsh's car was nowhere in sight. She turned accusing eyes on her mother. "You made him go. You didn't let him talk to me."

"Honey, he'll be back."

"When?" The question was pure challenge.

"Very soon. I promise. I told him I'd go and speak with him tonight, that we'd make plans for a time that you and he can get together."

Kim glared up at her mother, fire in her eyes. "Call him now, Mama. Tell him to come back right now. Tell him that I'm ready. Ready to get together."

Tory felt the self-indulgent tears again, pushing to spill over. She did not let them fall. She reached out, touched her daughter's silky hair.

The fire died in Kim's eyes, and defiance turned to a heartfelt plea. ''Mama. Please. Won't you just go ahead and call him now?''

There was only one answer. Tory gave it. ''Of course I will.''

Marsh was headed back to his hotel—no way he was going to try to deal with the old man right then—when his cell phone rang. He picked it up, flipped it open and pushed the talk button without even looking at the caller ID display.

Expecting to hear the voice of his manager at Boulevard, he growled, ''What?''

''Marsh.''

His stomach seemed to drop to his feet, that going-down-in-an-elevator feeling. ''Tory.''

''Marsh, I—''

''What? What is it? Talk to me.''

''There is a certain young lady here.'' Her voice had changed, gone tight, become oddly formal-sounding. ''A young lady who would really like to meet you.''

He couldn't quite let himself believe what she seemed to be saying. ''I...now?''

''Yes. Now.''

''I'll be right there.''

While she and Kim waited for Marsh to return, Tory called Lisa and asked her if she would please close up the shop by herself that evening. Kim sat on the stool across the kitchen counter when her mother made the call, watching and listening with desperate concentration, as if she didn't dare let Tory out of her sight. As if she feared that something might still happen to keep her father from appearing as promised—and that somehow her mother would be responsible when he didn't show.

Lisa said not to worry. Things were quiet. She could handle the store on her own, no problem.

"I wouldn't ask," said Tory, "but something pretty important has come up." Across the counter Kimmy's head bobbed up and down in emphatic agreement. Her burning eyes said it all—that what had come up was much more than just important. What had come up was everything that had ever mattered in the whole wide world.

"No problem," said Lisa. "I'll be all right."

Tory gave the clerk a quick rundown on what to do about the day's receipts. Then she said goodbye and hooked the phone back in its cradle on the wall.

Kimmy squirmed on the stool, her anticipation so acute her little body could barely contain it. "How long will it take him? How long till he gets here?"

"Not long, honey. A few minutes."

"You're sure? You're *sure* that he said that he would come?"

"I'm sure. He's coming."

"But what if—"

"Kimmy. He's coming. I promise you. He's coming right now."

"In a few minutes?"

"That's right."

Kim froze, all her senses straining. "What's that?" She jumped from the stool and sped through the double doors to the formal living/dining area at the front of the house. "It's him!" came the triumphant cry. "He's here!"

Her heart in her throat, Tory followed where her daughter had led, entering the big front room just in time to see Kim fly through the other set of doors that opened onto the entryway.

Kim had the front door flung back before Marsh was even out of the car. She leaned on the storm door, pushed it wide. And then she just stood there, wordless, frozen, staring at the man coming toward her up the walk.

Tory felt a cry snag in her throat. She wanted to go forward, to stand at her daughter's side for this. Every cell in her body seemed to scream at her to move. But something else—some wiser self—told her to stay where she was.

This was not her moment.

It was Kim's. And it was Marsh's.

He strode up the walk, his long, strong legs eating up the distance between him and the nine-year-old girl waiting at the door.

Tory looked at Kimmy. The child's slim body quivered, as if some unseen hand held her rooted in the doorway, though she strained to break free, to race for the man approaching up the walk.

Marsh reached her, stood for several endless heartbeats staring down at her.

Kim whispered, "You came. I knew you would. I've been waiting so long."

That was all Marsh needed. He held out his arms.

With a glad cry, Kimmy threw herself into them.

Chapter Five

After that initial embrace, Kim turned shy again.

For the next half hour she didn't seem to know what to say to Marsh.

But Tory had to give the man credit. He waited out the silence, accepting a 7UP from Tory, sitting in the family room with them, explaining to a wide-eyed Kim that he'd taken a room at a hotel not far away, but that he lived in Chicago, that he had his own company, a limousine service, and that he owned a big apartment in the city and a cabin by a lake and he hoped she'd be coming soon to visit him up north.

Tory waited with considerable anxiety for him to mention his sick father. But he must have realized that bringing up Blake would invite a lot of questions that neither he nor Tory were prepared to answer right then.

Kim was old enough to add two and two and get four on the subject of grandparents. She very well might wonder why she had never met the grandfather who lived less than ten miles from her house. But Marsh was careful. He only gave general information about his business and about his life.

Kim dared to ask, "Did you…get another family?"

"No, I'm still single."

"You don't have any other kids?"

"No, I do not."

Eventually, seeing how well Marsh was handling this, Tory began to relax.

So did Kim. She kicked off her sandals and gathered her legs up tight to her chest, so she could prop her chin on her cute knobby knees. And she started filling Marsh in on the world's most important subject: herself.

Soon enough, she was chattering away, apparently intent on sharing every detail of her life from birth to the present.

"I'm in third grade at Cleveland School, and when I graduate, in just three weeks, I'll be in fourth grade—well, I mean, first comes the summer. But you get to say you're in fourth grade as soon as third grade is over.

"I get *almost* straight As. 'Cept for math." She wrinkled her nose and shuddered, granting Marsh a sample of the reaction she reserved for unpleasant subjects—things like math and Brussels sprouts and cleaning her room. She sighed. "Sometimes I get Bs in math. I have three best friends—Sophie Johnson, Ivy Weaver and Alicia Sabatini. But Alicia is my *very* best friend, if you want to know the truth. Just don't tell Sophie and Ivy, that might hurt their feelings and I like them a lot, too. My favorite color is purple—like, duh, no kidding, huh? And yellow. I like yellow, too.

"I was a very cute little baby, ask Mama. I was hardly ever sick. We have lots of pictures of me, and you can look at them later. Oh. My teacher is Mrs. Cooper. Mrs. Cooper likes Garfield. You know, the cartoon cat? We have Garfield posters all over our room at school.

"And Rayanne usually takes care of me every day after school. She lives next door and she was best friends with my grandma Audra. But today Rayanne had to go shopping or something, so she couldn't watch me. My mom had to come home from the flower shop to get me.

"And you know what?" Kim stuck out her legs and jumped to a standing position. "I think you should see my room now. It's mostly yellow. Remember? One of my favorite colors. But don't worry. There is some purple, too. Mama and me put up a border with purple in it. And there's purple in the curtains. I think you'll like it. Will you come see?"

Marsh was already on his feet. "I'd like that very much."

Kim grabbed Marsh's index finger and began tugging him toward the hall. Marsh cast Tory a last bemused glance. Tory gave back an encouraging smile and remained in the family room, perched on the fat ottoman in front of the big easy chair, listening to her daughter's chatter fading off as she led her newly found father down the hall.

''I am going to show you my *whole* Beanie Baby collection. I have thirty-four of them, all still with the little tags on their ears. And my Barbies. Wait till you see my Barbies...''

They stayed in Kim's room for about twenty minutes. When they emerged, Kim dragged Marsh outside, ostensibly to show him her bicycle. They stayed out there for a lot longer than a look at a bicycle should have taken. Tory finally got impatient to see what they were up to.

When she went out to the backyard, though, she found them sitting on the iron bench beneath the fruitless mulberry tree, with Mr. Pickles, Kim's gray tabby cat, stretched out between them.

Kim petted the lounging cat and chattered on. ''I also play soccer. Did I tell you that? I play goalie, and it is not an easy job. You have to keep the other team from scoring, and if you don't, everyone on your own team gets mad at you. But I'm fast, Daddy. I'm pretty good...''

Marsh made an admiring, agreeable noise.

Kim looked up and saw her mother on the patio. ''We'll be in in a few minutes, Mama. But right now, we're *talking.*'' The second sentence was spoken with definite attitude.

Tory opened her mouth to remind her daughter of her manners—and shut it without uttering the rebuke. This was a special situation. Kim was trying to tell her father everything about herself, about her life, about her *world.* Maybe she had a right to show a little attitude when her mother had the bad judgment to interrupt.

Tory ducked back inside. By the time Kim and Marsh finally joined her a half hour later, it was four-thirty, and Tory had realized she needed to make a quick trip to the grocery store. Both Marsh and Kim urged her to go ahead. They'd be fine on their own.

Since they seemed to be doing so well together, Tory took them at their word. But as soon as she backed the car out of the garage and pushed the remote button that sent the door rumbling down, she became absolutely certain that she'd just made a giant-size error in judgment.

What could she have been thinking? For heaven's sake, she hardly knew Marsh anymore.

She drove to the supermarket and raced up and down the busy aisles, grabbing what she needed off the shelves and out of the meat case, agonizing the whole time over how she could possibly have been so foolish as to leave a virtual stranger alone with her child. The store was busy. It seemed she waited forever in the checkout line.

Finally, she paid the clerk and wheeled her groceries out to the car. She tossed the bags in the trunk, showing a complete lack of concern for bruiseable produce items, and shoved the empty cart in the general direction of the cart rack. She almost hit two other cars getting out of the parking lot. But at last she was back on the street, headed for home.

When she got there, she jumped from the car and ran in through the laundry room, anticipating hideous disasters that were no less dire for their vagueness.

She found Marsh and Tory sitting on the nubby green area rug at the big square coffee table in the family room. They were playing cards. They glanced her way in unison.

Marsh smiled and Kim said, ''We're playing U-No, Mama. And I'm winning.''

Tory's heart felt too big for her chest. She could see the resemblance between them so clearly right then—not only the dark, silky hair and almost-identical dark eyes, but also the tilt of the head, the sharply defined bow shape of the upper lip, the obstinate jut of the jaw.

They went back to their game—in unison, as they had turned toward her in the first place. Tory stared at their two dark heads, bent at matching angles, and felt that silly urge to cry again.

Marsh glanced up for the second time. ''Need some help with those groceries?''

''Oh. Oh, no. I can manage.''

''You're sure?''

She ordered her mouth to stretch into a bright smile. ''Positive.''

''Dad,'' Tory complained, ''you have to *concentrate.*''

''Sorry.'' He focused on his cards.

Tory brought in the groceries, put them away, got herself busy fixing a meat loaf.

They sat down to eat at six-thirty—the three of them. It had seemed only right to ask Marsh to stay. After they ate, Kim cleared the table and put the dishes in the dishwasher, with Marsh's help.

Then it was time for Kim to take care of her homework. Marsh, who showed no inclination to leave, helped her with her math and listened, rapt, as she read him the book report she'd gotten back from Mrs. Cooper just yesterday—the one with A-plus written on it in red ink.

At eight forty-five, Tory reminded Kim that it was time for her to take her shower and get ready for bed.

Kim immediately turned to Marsh. "You won't go anywhere, will you? You'll be here? To tuck me in?"

"Absolutely."

Kim ran to her room, grabbed her summer pajamas and disappeared into the hall bathroom, leaving Tory and Marsh alone to face a sudden awkwardness with each other. Now that it was just the two of them, Tory had no idea what to say to him—and he seemed to be pretty much at a loss himself.

Not that they didn't have plenty to talk about.

But right then was not the time. Kim could come flying out of the bathroom any minute, smelling of shampoo and toothpaste, eager for the thrilling first-time experience of having her father tuck her into bed.

"She's a great kid, Tory," Marsh said softly. "You've done a hell of a job with her."

Tory muttered a thank-you, thinking that it was just too bizarre. Marsh Bravo. Here, in her house, playing U-No with her daughter. Helping out with homework.

A voice in her head reproached, *Kim is* his *daughter, too....*

Tory suddenly remembered the load of laundry she'd been meaning to get into the washer that night. "Um. Listen, I have a few chores to take care of. The TV's in the front room, if you—"

"It's okay. I can amuse myself."

She stared at him, thinking how much he really had changed. He spoke like a man from a northern city now. His words had hard edges. And he carried himself differently. He held his head high.

The boy she had known had been hesitant, even shy—at least, with her. Adults then had called him sulky, brooding, said he had a bad attitude. But Tory had known better. Tory had known what he suffered, living with that awful daddy of his. And with her, he had always been sweet, tender and so very gentle.

Marsh—the grown-up, college-graduate, five-million-in-revenues-a-year Marsh—narrowed his eyes at her. "What are you staring at?"

"I...nothing. Just thinking."

"About what?" The question was pure challenge.

She wanted to lie—and to edge around him, get out from under the piercing regard of those eyes. But she held her ground and she told the truth. "About you. About how much you've changed."

"How much is that?"

"Well, I would have to say, a lot."

"And that's bad, right? I'm not the boy you knew."

"I didn't say it was bad."

"No. But you thought it."

She backed up a step. Why, they were practically arguing. How had they gone from what a great job she was doing with Kim—to this?

Stress, she thought. We're both under a lot of stress. This is not any easier for him than it is for me.

She strove for an even tone. "Marsh, look. Let's not...push each other. Having you here, it's...well,

I'm sure it's not easy for you. And it's hard for me, too.''

Those dark eyes regarded her. Right then they were a long way from the tender eyes she remembered. Right then they were hard as black rock. ''Yeah. Imagine. Me. In your daddy's house, sitting down at the table to *eat* with you. Incredible.''

The gibe hit home.

She *had* loved him. With all of her heart. She would have run away with him, if only he would have taken her. But her parents had never approved of him. They said she could do better than ''that troubled Bravo boy.''

So most of the time she'd had with Marsh had been stolen time. She would sneak out to be with him, lie to her parents, get her friends to cover for her. When he did come to the house, he never came in. If he came in the daytime, it was only to mow the lawn. And when he came at night, he would tap quietly on her bedroom window. She would meet him outside.

Never once, until tonight, had he sat down to share a meal at her table.

He said coldly, ''We have a lot to talk about.''

As if she didn't know that—as if she could do anything about it right now. ''When Kimmy's in bed.''

''Just so we're clear on the evening's agenda.''

''We're clear.'' She thought of his mean old daddy, lying in his hospital bed. ''What about your father, though? Should you be—''

''Don't worry about him. I'll see him in the morning. I've left instructions at the hospital. If something important comes up, they'll call.''

She thought of her laundry again. Better get to it. No point in standing here waiting for outright war to break out. "And now I really have to—"

"Right. Those chores."

"Yes. Excuse me." She slid around him and took off down the hall.

Twenty minutes later the load of laundry had reached the spin cycle and Kim was all dressed in her purple sleep shirt with Barbie's picture on the front of it.

"I brushed my teeth," she announced. "And I used the dental floss like I'm s'posed to. So, please, will you both come in and kiss me good-night?"

Tory had planned to let Marsh do the honors on his own. But what mother could resist such a sweet request? She trooped down the hall in the rear, Marsh ahead of her and Kim leading the way.

In her purple-accented yellow room, Kim yanked back the covers and jumped into bed. She lay back on her yellow pillow and let out a big, contented sigh.

"My family." She was beaming, looking from Marsh to Tory and back to Marsh again. "Together at last..."

Words of caution rose to Tory's lips: Slow down here, young lady. Let's take this one step at a time....

Tory held those words back. It seemed wrong, somehow, to speak of caution now. Kim had finally met her father. And in spite of the tension between Marsh and Tory, the meeting had gone beautifully—much better than Tory would have dared to dream.

The rest they would work out—starting as soon as she and Marsh left this room.

Kim's expression had turned solemn. Tory probably should have guessed what was coming. Kim said, "I've been thinking. About the wedding. I want to be the maid of honor. I think I'm old enough, I really, really do."

Tory could have kicked herself for not speaking up a moment before. "Whoa." She forced a laugh. "Slow down, girl. Not so fast."

But Kim wouldn't take the hint—and Tory probably shouldn't have expected her to. This was, after all, her daughter's dream come true. Kim's fondest wish had always been to be part of what she called a "regular" family, which would include not only herself and her mother, but also her father, and, eventually, a little sister—and maybe even a brother, though Kim was never 100 percent sure about the brother.

Kim spoke sternly. "Mama. You and Daddy have a *daughter.* You never got married. That's not right and you know it. People who have children *should* be married—and Daddy *said* he didn't get another family, so you and him can get married, and everything will be perfect."

"Wait just a minute, here," Tory began, matching her daughter in sternness. Unfortunately, she couldn't quite make up her mind how to go on from there.

Marsh came to her rescue. "Kim." He sat on the edge of the bed. "It's been a great afternoon. I loved every minute of it."

"Me, too. I'm so glad you're home. And I want you to—"

He reached out, put a finger to the mouth that was so much like his own. "Listen to me. You are nine years old. There are a lot of decisions you just don't get to make."

"What does that *mean?*" Kim demanded. "You're not going to marry Mom?"

"It means there are a lot of things to consider here." Good Lord, the man didn't miss a beat. Tory marveled at him, the bad boy she'd once loved, grown up into a diplomat. "Your mother and I have to do some serious talking."

"What you have to do is get *married.*"

He shook his head. "You're not listening."

Kim let out a small, wounded cry. "I am so."

"Good." He gently smoothed the silky bangs away from her forehead. "I can't tell you, right this minute, and neither can your mother, what is going to happen. You just have to wait."

"How *long* do I have to wait?"

"Not too long."

"Till tomorrow? In the morning? While we're having breakfast? Can we talk about the wedding then?"

Marsh shifted on the edge of the bed. Tory read the body language. The barrage of questions would wear even a diplomat down. He wasn't sure how to go on from there.

Tory stepped up. She put her hand on his shoulder. Through the cloth of his shirt she felt the heat and the muscle. It struck her like a blow—it was the first time she had touched him in ten full years.

He turned, looked at her, one dark brow arching in

question. It was too much, meeting those eyes of his and touching him, too. She dropped her hand away.

"Say good-night, Marsh," she instructed with a firmness that surprised her. "Kim, give your father a kiss."

Kim started to sit up. "But—"

Tory looked at her steadily. "Not another word."

Kim subsided onto her pillow, her expression talking mutiny, but her mouth thankfully shut. She lifted her face for Marsh's kiss.

He brushed his lips against her forehead. "Good night." Rising, he moved back to make room for Tory.

Kim sniffed and nobly offered her mother her cheek.

"Night, honey," Tory whispered as she bent close.

Kim said nothing. Tory knew her game. If pressed, she would argue, "You told me 'not another word....'"

So Tory didn't press. She straightened and tipped her head toward the hallway. Marsh picked up the signal and turned to go. Tory followed after him, pausing to switch off the light and pull the door closed.

"Do you...can I get you some coffee, or something?" Tory offered, once the two of them were alone in the family room.

"No, thanks. I'm fine."

She realized that the washer had stopped. "I... maybe I should put the clothes in the dryer."

She saw suspicion in his eyes, as if he thought her laundry was only a ploy to put off the inevitable.

And maybe it was.

After a moment he shrugged. "Sure. Do it."

She swept out a hand. "Have a seat, why don't you?" There was a sofa, the easy chair, the recliner. He could have his pick.

"Just deal with the laundry, all right?"

"Fine."

She left him, striding purposefully through the kitchen and out to where the washer waited. She moved the clothes into the dryer and turned the dial. The dryer began rumbling.

And then she had no reason to avoid going back to the family room.

She rejoined him. "Well. I suppose we ought to..."

He smiled, but it wasn't a very warm smile. "Get this over with?"

"Yes. I guess so." Not that she had a clue where to begin.

He asked, in a low tone, "Are you sure she'll stay in bed now?"

"She should."

"*Should* isn't good enough. I don't want her listening in."

He sounded so grim. Grim and determined. His not-very-warm smile was gone altogether now. Her stomach went into knot formation. What was he planning? Did he mean to try and take Kimmy away from her?

Dear Lord, let that not be so.

She didn't think he could get custody, could tear Kimmy away from the home she had known all her life. But the courts were much stronger now, on the side of the father. And he had gone and made a fortune. He'd have plenty of money to spend on lawyers.

He could provide for Kim. He would surely get joint custody, at least, if he fought hard enough.

And why shouldn't he *have* joint custody? If he was willing to provide for his daughter, and to give her time and attention while she stayed with him?

Today he had seemed very attentive. Like a man who would make an excellent father...

It came to Tory again right then, this time with certainty, the thought barreling down on her like a runaway train: their lives, from this day, would be so much changed.

He must have picked up something of the anguish she felt. He spoke more gently than before. "Are you all right?"

She did the breathing thing, slow and carefully. And she swallowed. "Yes. I'm just...a little overwhelmed by all this, I guess. But I'll get through it." She suggested, "We could go out in back, sit on the patio. No way she can hear us from out there. And we can see in the window, in case she wanders out here."

"Good idea." He went to the door, opened it, waited for her to go through ahead of him.

They sat at the glass-topped patio table, in the comfortably cushioned patio chairs. It was a warm night, but not overly so. Tory left the patio lights off. Enough of a glow bled through the windows for their purposes. And the dark was comforting, easier on Tory's overworked nerves. Crickets sang in the grass, and the night birds called from the mulberry tree.

Marsh sat back in the cushioned chair and rested his hand on the nubby glass of the table. Tory looked at that hand, in order not to have to look directly at him.

But of course, that hand was every bit as dangerous to look at as all the other parts of him. All the parts that were so different—and yet somehow too much the same.

"Last night," he said. "When you ran out..."

She nodded, still staring hard at that hand. "I didn't know. How to tell you. It was all so sudden. I made a big mess of it."

"It's all right." His voice, through the darkness, was low, soothing. Something just next door to tender. A lot like the voice of the boy she had loved. "I understand."

Gratitude washed through her. Maybe it would all work out.

Somehow. "I...thank you. For that."

He pulled his hand back, laid it on the arm of his chair. She didn't follow it with her gaze, just continued staring at the empty place where it had been.

He said, "Is there...anyone special now? A man that you're seeing?"

She had started to relax a little—but his question made her tense up all over again. "I told you last night—"

"You said you weren't married, but you didn't tell me if—"

"No. There's no one...special, as you put it."

She waited. For him to say more. But he said nothing. She found herself elaborating. "I...date, now and then, go out, casually, to a movie, or to dinner. But it's nothing..." Nothing *what?* She thought desperately, her mind suddenly as blank as a bleached white sheet. The word finally came. "...serious. Nothing serious."

She felt his eyes, watching. Somehow, she couldn't quite meet them.

"I'm happy," she said, defiance creeping in. "As I am. Just Kim. And me."

"Happy," he repeated, as if he didn't trust that word or its meaning.

"Yes. Happy." She raised her chin. "And I... Look. What does it matter, if I date, if I'm happy? We have to discuss Kimmy. We have to decide what we're going to do."

"We will. But first I'd like to...catch up on a few things."

"What things? You need to know who I go out with?"

"I was just curious, that's all." He kept on looking at her. She could feel his gaze. It seemed to draw on her, to compel her to look back at him.

"What?" she demanded, giving in, meeting his eyes.

He asked in a tone that accused, "Why didn't you try to tell me that I had a daughter?"

She frowned at him. Hadn't they gone over that already? "I...I said, it was such a shock, your showing up, calling out of nowhere. You just told me you understood."

"I'm not talking about last night. I'm talking about over the last nine or ten years."

"I don't...the last nine or ten years?"

"Yes. Why didn't you come looking for me?"

"What are you talking about?"

"You know what I'm talking about. You've had my daughter for almost a decade. And it seems to me you've expended minimal effort to let me in on the news."

Outrage. Oh, she could feel it. Burning all through her. It took every ounce of will she possessed to keep her voice low. "I do not believe this, Marsh Bravo. How can you ask me that?"

He only looked at her, his strong jaw set and his eyes as unknowable as the dark side of the moon.

She wanted to jump on him, to slap his hard, accusing face. "*You* never called, *you* never wrote—except that one letter to tell me to forget you. I wrote to you. More than once. And in *my* letters, I told you everything. And you…you sent my letters back to me. You didn't even bother to open them and read them. If you had, you would have known about the daughter you're accusing me of keeping from you."

She waited, feeling slightly breathless and extremely self-righteous, for him to say how sorry he was that he had presumed to ask such an insensitive question.

She didn't get what she waited for. He said, "All right. That takes care of the first six or seven months after I left. But what about the other nine and a half years? You might have tried a letter or two in that time."

She gaped at him. "Along with your money and your college degree, you have developed a lot of nerve, Marsh Bravo. You got what you asked for. Why are you badgering me?"

"You know why. Because I didn't have all the information."

"You had all the information you *wanted,* that's for sure. And anyway, those letters weren't all I did."

"What else?"

She stared at him, through the darkness. Something in his shadowed face said he already knew what else. But she told him, anyway.

"I went to that father of yours."

He swore, low, with feeling. "I knew it."

She probably should have left it at that. But she couldn't, not after the way he'd accused her just now. She wanted him to feel a little of what she had felt back then, to realize how bad it had been for her.

"I was so scared, to go see that evil man in that creepy shack of his out there in the woods. But I went. I was far gone then. Seven months along. And I was desperate to find you. Your father...he came out on the porch, with his shotgun in his hands. He pointed those two barrels right at me. I stood there, shakin', thinking that maybe he was just mean enough to go ahead and shoot me—and not sure if I cared if he did.

"I said, 'I need to find Marsh, Mr. Bravo. I am going to have his baby and he needs to know that.'

"He lowered the shotgun then. And he laughed at me. He said he didn't know where you were, and even if he did, he wouldn't tell me. That I should take myself and my little unborn bastard and get off his property. I begged him some more. And he laughed some more. And then he just went back inside and shut the door and left me standing there."

Tory shivered, and her shivering had nothing to do

with the temperature. "So maybe, if you want to blame somebody for not telling you about Kim, you ought to go talk to that old man in the hospital. He knew almost from the first that you were going to be a father. And he also must have figured out how to get in touch with you, since he somehow got hold of you to let you know he was at death's door."

Marsh made a harsh, scoffing sound. "You think it's going to do me any damn good to get on him for the hopeless SOB he is and always has been? He's beyond hope. I think you know that."

"So you blame me instead?"

He was silent for a long time, so long she almost thought he wasn't going to answer her. At last he said, "I guess I expected more from you."

"You expected way too much."

"Maybe I did."

"You never came back, in all those years. I wasn't hiding, Marsh. I was right here all the time."

"Tory, you had my child. Kim changes everything. You know that she does."

"Oh, come on. What if I *had* kept trying to find you? You really think I would have succeeded? It's not that easy to find someone when you don't have any idea where they might have gone."

"I'd just like you to say it, Tory. I'd like it right out in the open. You gave up on me, you wiped me out of your life, and you did it years and years ago."

"Because you *wanted* me to. You wrote me and told me to forget about you. You didn't answer my letters. You *disappeared.*"

He was the one who looked away then. He stared off toward the high fence at the back of the yard.

They both were silent. The crickets sang.

Finally he said, "This isn't getting us anywhere, is it?"

She swallowed. "No, it is not."

"I should have read your letters."

Her heart melted when he said that. She had to swallow again.

He said, "We lost something, Tory. Something so special. Something innocent and pure."

She knew exactly what he meant. Love. So precious and rare. They had known love. Together. And they each had made certain choices. And those choices had changed them. They were two different people now.

The love they'd shared was lost to them, a bittersweet memory, no longer vivid. No longer quite real. As if it had happened to two other people.

She confessed, "You're right. I should have kept trying. To find you. I know that. It ended up being easier, just to work on forgetting."

He turned those eyes on her again. She saw the pain in them, saw the loss. Saw her baby, who was his baby, too. The baby who had so quickly become a plump toddler, then a little girl in a new dress, heading off for her first day in kindergarten. Then, out of nowhere, a girl who could write her name in cursive, could add and subtract. Divide. Multiply. Could dive for a soccer ball, and capture it before it hit the net...

Poor Marsh. He had missed so much. And none of it would ever come again.

He said, in a voice that caught on a ragged breath,

"I'm here now, Tory. And I'm not just going to go away. We're going to have to work together now, at least when it comes to taking care of Kim."

"I understand that. I honestly do. I—"

A phone started ringing: Marsh's cell phone.

He pulled it from a pocket, flipped it open. "This is Marsh Bravo." He listened. "How bad?" The voice on the other end of the line spoke again. Marsh said, "All right. Thank you." He flipped the thing shut.

She knew what it must be. "Your father?"

Marsh nodded. "He's had another heart attack. They don't think he'll make it this time."

If there was anyone in the whole world Tory Winningham could say she hated, it would have to be Blake Bravo. Still, her heart contracted at the thought that he might die. A death, even of a wicked man, was still a death. A sad proof of what we all come to.

Marsh stood. He slid the phone back into the pocket he'd taken it from. "I have to go to the hospital."

"Yes." Tory rose from her own chair.

But then he just stood there, looking bewildered. "What am I saying? I don't *have* to go. And I sure as hell don't want to go. If he *doesn't* die this time, I'll be tempted to kill him."

"Marsh. Don't talk like that."

He made a scoffing sound. "I was so damn afraid, remember, of him coming after me, to get his revenge for the way I finally gave him a little of what he'd been giving me all my life?"

"Yes. I do remember."

"He never came. And now we know why."

"Marsh..."

"We know what his revenge was. To let me go all this time, without knowing—" his voice trailed off, but then he found it again "—about Kim."

Tory said what she thought he needed to hear right then. "No matter what he's done, he's still your daddy."

Marsh made no reply to that, which was just as well, in Tory's opinion. They went inside and she walked him through the house to the front door, where he turned to her.

"We haven't...decided anything, really." His mouth kicked up at one corner in something that almost resembled a smile. "Kim will be mad at us."

"Too bad."

"Tomorrow?"

"Yes. Call me."

"I'll do that."

She wished him well, watched him hurry down the dark walk to his car.

Alone, she thought. He looks so alone.

That didn't seem right, somehow. That he should go to face whatever waited at the hospital all on his own. A man should have family around, when his father—even a father like Blake Bravo—was dying. Someone to lean on, if he needed it. Someone to talk to if talking might help.

"Oh, don't be a darn fool," she said to the beveled glass in the top of her front door. "You are not Marsh Bravo's family."

But she *had* loved him once. And they *did* have a child together. And it had been a tough enough day for him already, what with finding out about Kim.

And what family did Marsh have—other than his terrible daddy, which was probably worse than having no family at all? Who would stand beside him now, when he needed a loved one—or even a friend—the most?

This is not my problem, Tory told herself. It has nothing at all to do with me.

But no matter how much she lectured herself to the contrary, in her heart she knew that Marsh needed someone at his side. And right then she was the only someone available.

Chapter Six

Blake was in surgery when Marsh reached the hospital. So he sat in a room with mauve walls and black padded chairs, thumbing through a dog eared *Sports Illustrated,* waiting for further word on his father's condition.

He'd been sitting there for about twenty minutes when he glanced up and saw Tory walking toward him.

For a second he thought he must be mistaken. But no. It was Tory. Wearing the same trim white shirt and slim sky-blue slacks she'd had on earlier that evening.

He dropped the magazine and stood. ''Kim?''

''She's fine. I took her next door, to Rayanne Pickett's.''

He pictured Rayanne Pickett's unsmiling face in his

mind. She had never liked him. She and Tory's mother had always been the best of friends, and they both thought Marsh Bravo was way beneath the Winninghams' precious only child.

"What are you doing here?" he demanded, in a voice harsher than he meant it to be.

Tory didn't take offense. She just smiled. And she touched him. It was the second time she'd done that since he'd forced himself back into her life. The other time had been in Kim's bedroom. She'd put her hand on his shoulder—and then quickly pulled it away.

This time she grasped his arm. Her hand was warm. It was one of those touches meant to steady the person being touched. And it worked. He felt better, just at that small contact.

She said, "This seemed like something you shouldn't go through alone. You should have a friend with you."

A friend? Was that what she was now? What she wanted to be?

That seemed...hopeful. And sad, at the same time.

She asked, looking sheepish. "Would you like me to go?"

Hell, no. "Why would I want that?"

"Good. Then I'll stay."

He thought about Rayanne Pickett's frowning face again. "What did you tell that Pickett woman?"

"The truth. That your daddy is probably dying and I didn't think you ought to be alone."

"I'll bet she's on the phone with your mother right now, sharing the news that bad Marsh Bravo is back in town and you've run off in the middle of the night to—''

''Offer a shoulder to lean on during a tough time.'' Tory was looking reproachful. ''As a matter of fact, Bayonne was very understanding.''

''I'll bet.''

''And she'll take good care of Kim. Kim can stay all night if need be. So I think we should just be grateful she was available and forget about her for now. We should concentrate on...the business at hand.''

It sounded like pretty good advice to him. He let out a breath he hadn't even realized he was holding. ''Thank you. For doing this.''

She touched him again, a little pat, higher up on the arm this time. ''Let's sit down.''

So they sat. And they waited. It didn't take all that long.

The surgeon Marsh had spoken to the previous day came out to find him at a little before eleven. At the sight of the doctor in green hospital scrubs, face mask still dangling around his neck, Tory reached for Marsh's hand. He gave it to her. And he held on tight. They stood as one.

He knew what was coming. He could see it in the surgeon's bleak expression.

''Mr. Bravo. I'm so sorry...''

The doctor said that Blake had died. A massive coronary thrombosis: a blood clot in the heart.

He said the things that doctors always say. ''We did all we could. Would to God we could have done more.''

Marsh watched the man's mouth move, saying all

the right things, telling him that his father's body would be released in a few hours to the funeral home—and if Marsh hadn't taken care of finding a funeral home, he ought to do that now.

Marsh said nothing. He held on to Tory's hand and he waited. Until the doctor at last stopped listing his regrets and asked him a question.

"Would you like to see him?"

Marsh stepped back, but there was nowhere to go. He felt his calves come up against the seat behind him. "See him? What for?"

The doctor made more understanding noises. Some people wanted a few minutes alone with the deceased. The doctor always liked to give family members that choice, if at all possible.

"No," said Marsh, picturing his father's face, slack-jawed, vacant, the mad-wolf eyes staring blankly. "I don't want to see him."

Of course, said the doctor. No problem. He understood.

"Thank you," Marsh was finally able to say politely. The doctor took his free hand, squeezed it. Marsh squeezed back. It seemed like the right thing to do.

The doctor turned to go—and Marsh couldn't quite let him. "Wait."

The doctor stopped, glanced back. "Yes?"

"I think I had better see the body, after all." He felt Tory's hand tighten in his. He squeezed back.

"Of course," said the doctor. "This way."

Marsh knew he had no right to ask Tory to go with him. He should have pulled his hand from hers, said it was okay. She could stay here. No need for her to see this.

But he said nothing. He gripped her hand tight. Side-by-side they followed the doctor to the room where his father's body lay.

He stood over the still figure, looked down at the face that sometimes, even now, turned his dreams to nightmares. The eyes were closed, thank God.

But there was no doubt. The dead man was Blake Bravo.

Crazy, but Marsh had needed to see it for himself.

He turned from the unmoving figure on the bed. ''That's all. Let's go.'' He led Tory out of that room.

Next, there were forms to sign; he made sure that his father's hospital bills would be sent to him. And he called a funeral home, one that was right down the street. They would come and get his father's body as soon as it was released. And he was to go over there in the morning, to make the arrangements.

''Cremation,'' Marsh said into the phone. ''He wanted to be cremated. He didn't want a funeral.''

The pleasant voice on the other end of the line told him he could take care of all that in the morning.

He muttered another thank-you and hung up the phone.

By then it was midnight. He signed another paper to receive his father's ''valuables'' and an orderly gave him a big plastic bag with Blake's things inside. And that was it. There was no more reason to hang around the hospital.

Tory said, ''Follow me back to my house. I'll make

coffee. I can even offer you a stiff shot of whisky, if that's more to your liking right now."

The whisky sounded good. Probably too good. "I'll take the coffee."

"Then come on. Let's go."

He followed behind her dark-green sedan, with the sliver of new moon high in the sky seeming to lead them on. The streets were quiet, so late on a weekday. Even the college kids had settled in at their dorms and fraternity houses for the night. The trip took only a few minutes.

When Tory swung into her driveway, she sent both of the twin garage doors rolling up. He took that as a signal and pulled into the vacant spot next to hers. The doors rolled down again. That gray cat of Kim's was sitting on the washing machine giving itself a leisurely bath when Tory led him in through the laundry room.

That gray cat of Kim's...

Kim.

My daughter. Kim. His mind seemed to get hung up there, on the name, on the new and shocking concept of her connection to him. It seemed somehow significant that he should have learned he had a child on the same day that the old man had died.

Significant. Yes. That was the word for it.

Though he couldn't decide exactly why.

Tory's keys made a bright clinking sound as she hung them on a little hook just inside the kitchen door.

Keys.

He recalled the old man, yesterday, ordering him to take his keys, to stay at the shack out east of town.

The keys would be in the bag of personal effects Marsh had brought from the hospital.

But hell if Marsh would ever use them. That damn shack could cave in on itself. He was never going out there. He was free of that place, for good and all.

"Make yourself at home," Tory said.

She went and dropped her purse on the sideboard built into the section of wall that joined the kitchen to the open family room. Then she returned to the main part of the kitchen and flicked on a set of under-the-cabinet lights. He watched as she took out a can of coffee and began spooning grounds into the coffee maker. She glanced his way. He was still standing right where she'd left him, in the open doorway to the laundry room.

"Sit down, Marsh," she said, in the way a woman might speak to a not-too-bright child—gently, but with firmness.

He felt no irritation, that she spoke to him as if he were a child, only a kind of ironic amusement. He did as she instructed, going around the section of counter that jutted out between the breakfast table and the sink, sliding onto a stool. He watched her as she filled the carafe and poured its contents into the reservoir.

She pushed the button to start the brewing cycle, then put the coffee can back in the cupboard. "It'll just be a few minutes."

He shrugged, listening to the gurgling sound of the coffeemaker, thinking that it was a reassuring sound. Soothing. The kind of sound that seemed to say all was right with the world.

Whether it really was right or not.

"Marsh." She came and leaned on the other side of the counter, elbows on the cream-colored tiles, looking sweet and worried. The lights under the cabinet made her red hair shine, put a glow on those freckles sprinkled over her nose. "You seem so quiet."

He didn't respond to that, but asked instead, "Should you go next door and get Kim?"

She glanced at the digital clock on the stove. "It's late. Rayanne has probably gone to bed. I'll let them both sleep and go get her first thing in the morning."

He didn't know whether he liked that, his daughter staying all night at that Pickett woman's. But he kept his mouth shut about it. Kim had spoken of the woman as if she were some sort of honorary grandmother. And Tory obviously thought highly of her.

Tory was looking at him, real concern for him in her eyes.

He wished she would touch him again. He didn't feel all that bad, really. Just a little bit...removed from himself. Not quite all there. He had the sense that if she touched him he would come back into himself again. He would feel okay. Right. Grounded. A part of the world again, the world that included this kitchen and this woman, with her red hair and the sweet freckles on her nose.

She granted his wish—without him even telling her it was in his mind. He had folded his hands on the counter. She reached across and put her right hand over his joined ones.

He looked down at where she touched him, then into her deep-blue eyes, shadowed by lashes that were red as the hair on her head—lashes that were not especially long, but very thick. He remembered vaguely that he used to like to put his mouth to them, to feel them, brushing, against his lips.

She said his name again, "Marsh?" and somehow made it another inquiry into his state of mind.

He thought of the old man again.

Something must have shown in his face, because she then gave his hands a little squeeze and asked, "What?"

He told her. "Somebody ought to miss him, some one person in the whole damn world. But I don't think there's anyone out there who's going to feel anything stronger than a mild tug of sadness to hear that he's gone. And that sadness is only because he was a human being and it's sad that we all have to go sometime." He felt a smile then, a wry one, pulling at the corner of his mouth. "At least, I *think* he was a human being—and maybe there are some who will feel more than sadness. Maybe some will feel relief. Maybe some will even be glad. I don't know. The truth is, aside from the way he tortured me and my mother, I don't know much about him. He was always... dropping hints. He'd claim he came from a rich family, out in Southern California. Or that he had cousins, ranchers, in Wyoming. And another cousin in New York. To hear him tell it, he had cousins all over the country—sometimes, anyway. Then if you caught him on another day, he'd swear he was the last of his line. And he used to say he'd done things, big things, *bad* things. And he'd gotten away with them. And yesterday, out of nowhere, he told me he'd had a brother who died of a stroke.''

"An uncle,'' she said. "I never even knew you had an uncle.''

"That's the point, Tory. I probably don't. Who the hell knows? Only the old man. And he would never say for certain. Now, he *can't* say at all.''

"So sad.'' Slowly she shook that red head, the light catching on certain strands, some gold, some strawberry, some deep, rich auburn. Her hand felt so good, cupped lightly over both of his. He hoped she'd leave it there, for a while at least. She showed no sign that she meant to remove it.

She said, "I heard you tell them at the funeral parlor that he didn't want a funeral.''

"That's right.''

"So what then?''

"I'm supposed to have the body cremated, then take his ashes out and dump them in Lake Thunderbird.''

Those auburn brows drew together. "No kind of service at all?''

"That's what he wanted. And that's all right with me. Probably better than some funeral that no one would come to.''

She idly rubbed her hand back and forth over his folded ones. "You think that no one would come? No one at all?''

"Hell. I don't know. I know he said no funeral, and I guess that'll have to be enough.''

The coffeemaker gave out an extra loud gurgling sputter. She glanced over her shoulder at it. "Coffee's ready.''

Without stopping to think about what he was doing, he caught her hand before she could pull it away. She let out a small, tight sound of surprise and she turned back to him again, auburn brows arching in question.

He let go. "Sorry."

There was color in her pale skin, a soft blush beneath the freckles. "What, Marsh?"

"Nothing. It was...comforting, that's all. The feel of your hand."

"Oh. Well." She flashed him a shy grin and turned to get mugs from the cabinet above the built-in sideboard. She took a pair of spoons from a drawer. "I don't believe I recall how you take your coffee."

"We were teenagers," he said. "We didn't do a lot of coffee drinking."

"You liked Mountain Dew. I remember that. And Jolt cola."

"Yeah. Even then I knew where to look for the caffeine."

She set one of the spoons on the counter in front of him, placing it just so, with the handle toward him, her head tipped down as she concentrated on the small task. He could see the natural part, at the top of her head, the line of tender pale skin where the hair separated.

The scent of her came to him. She wore a perfume that smelled a little like geraniums. And roses. And maybe cinnamon. It was an intriguing, attractive scent, spicy and fresh at the same time.

Had she smelled the same ten years ago?

He couldn't remember. He just knew he liked the scent of her now.

"Marsh? What can I get you? For your coffee?"

"Just sugar."

She brought down a white sugar bowl, set it a few inches from his spoon. Then she took the two mugs over to the coffeepot.

She filled the cups. He watched her—the tumble of curly red hair, the straight, slim line of her back, the soft outward curves of her hips.

She returned to his side of the kitchen, bearing the two full mugs. She set his mug before him and took a sip from hers. He did what was expected of him, spooning in sugar, stirring, sipping.

It didn't take long to drink it all.

"More?" she asked.

"No." He pushed the mug aside, slid off the stool. "I should get going."

"You're sure?"

Sure? What did that mean? He wasn't particularly sure about anything at that point. "Why? Are you asking me to stay?"

Her eyes widened. "Well, no. I wasn't. But I do have a spare room. You're welcome to—"

"Tory. It's okay. Thanks for the coffee. And for… being there tonight."

"You are very welcome." She trailed behind him to the front of the house, slipping ahead of him when they got there, turning the dead bolt and pulling the big door wide. "Good night. Drive carefully, please. Now that my daughter has a father, I'd like her to, um, keep him for a while."

He looked out at the sloping front walk—and remembered that he'd left his car in the garage.

She must have realized it, too, at the same moment that he did. She giggled, a sweet, girlish sound. "Oops. I guess you'll need that car of yours."

She shut the door, turned the bolt and maneuvered around him again. He fell in step behind her, his gaze where it probably shouldn't have been: on the gentle swaying of her hips.

He thought about that giggle. Like the scent of her perfume, the sound of her giggle had been lost to him. It was a whole new experience, hearing it now. It stirred no faint echoes of old memories—only a very current, very real, very male interest.

That hurt, somehow. As if by not remembering the scent or the laugh of the Tory he had known, he had betrayed what they had once shared, proved it to be less than he'd always believed.

Kim's cat was asleep on the dryer now, all curled into itself. Tory opened the door that led to the garage. She pressed a button. A light went on and one of the twin garage doors—the one behind his rental car—began its rumbling rise. She went on, around the back of her car, then between her car and his, until she reached his driver's door.

She turned to him, waiting for him to slide behind the wheel, so that she could wish him yet another good-night and then stand there waving as he backed away.

He looked at her wide, soft mouth and he couldn't help wondering.

Would her kiss be the same?

Did he even remember it—the taste of her mouth, the feel of her body under his hands?

Yes.

Damn it.

He did remember.

Or at least he remembered that at one time the taste of her, the *feel* of her had been everything to him.

"Um." She coughed. "Well." She folded her arms across her middle, a move that he recognized as a defensive one. "Listen. If there's anything I can do..."

She shouldn't have said that. It was exactly the wrong thing to say.

Or maybe exactly the *right* thing, depending on how a man wanted to look at it.

"As a matter of fact, there is."

She looked sweetly surprised. She hadn't expected him to give her that answer. Her offer had just been one of those things a woman says. *If I can help... Whatever I can do...* He hid his knowing smile and he leaned closer, just marginally, to see how she'd react.

She held her ground, schooled her expression to one of helpful determination. "Good. Tell me. Whatever it is, I'll be glad to—"

He told her. "You can kiss me."

Chapter Seven

Tory could not quite believe he had said that.

Kiss him?

It was so...inappropriate.

His father had just *died*, for heaven's sake. And she had gone to him at the hospital strictly in a *friendly* capacity. Certainly he couldn't be thinking that she—

That they—

Oh, good gravy. She did feel flustered. She hadn't a clue what to say to him, standing there so...broad-shouldered and handsome, possessing the same eyes and the same mouth as the boy she had once loved, and yet seeming to be someone else altogether.

Someone so different.

Someone a little bit dangerous in a way that *her* Marsh had never been dangerous. Because *her* Marsh had been just that: hers. Utterly and completely, right from the first.

Her Marsh had been shaking, the first time he dared to kiss her. She had smiled, against his mouth, feeling a wonderful, womanly power and reveling in it.

This Marsh, well, he sure wasn't shaking, and she had a feeling, if he kissed her, that she'd be more likely to sigh or moan than to smile.

She realized she was staring at his mouth, which had turned up at the corners in a far too knowing grin. She jerked her gaze upward—to those eyes, which were watching her, looking *into* her, it felt like, in a way she didn't think she approved of one bit.

"Marsh, I don't think that we—"

He shrugged, as if the whole thing was terribly casual, terribly *minor.* "You asked if you could do anything for me."

"Well, yes, but I didn't mean—"

"Didn't you?"

She huffed in a breath. "You could do me the courtesy of letting me finish my own sentences."

He shrugged again. "Have at it."

"I beg your pardon."

"Finish yourself a few sentences."

"Well, I just— That is, I only— Will you *please* stop looking so amused?"

He tipped his head to the side, considering. And then he said, "Good night." He pulled open his car door. She had to back away a little to make room. He climbed in behind the wheel and started to pull the door closed.

She shouldn't have, she knew it. But she stepped forward and grabbed onto the door. "Oh, Marsh..."

He leaned out, just a little, and looked up into her eyes. "What?"

It was a bad idea and it was inappropriate and crazy and probably just plain wrong. It could complicate what was already more than complicated enough.

But then again, it was only a kiss.

And there was one way that this Marsh was just like the old Marsh. They both—the old and the new Marsh—excited her.

She *wanted* to kiss him. She wanted it a lot. For different reasons, maybe, than she had wanted to kiss him then.

Back then when she kissed him, she had felt so...beautiful. So powerful in that special, womanly way.

Now, she felt...scared. Yes. Scared and anticipatory. Like someone about to attempt a risky, thrilling act. To dive off a high diving board, bungee jump or parachute from an airplane.

She did not feel powerful as she had in the past. But the *desire* for his kiss—that she felt now just as urgently as she had felt it all those years ago.

"All right," she said.

"I can see this is a big sacrifice for you."

She scowled down at him. "Are we going to keep talking about it? Because if we are, I'm sure we can talk ourselves out of—"

He cut her off again, right in the middle of her sentence. He surged upward and pressed that mouth of his to hers.

She moaned.

And then she sighed.

And then she gave a little cry and yanked her mouth away. The garage door behind his car was wide open. Where they were standing, anyone walking by on the street could have seen them.

She started to shut his car door.

He didn't let her. He held it open.

Then he got out of the car.

She put a hand out. "No. Marsh..."

But he showed no inclination to listen to her. She backed toward the rear of her car and he came with her, like some invisible string was pulling him along, moving him with her, step for careful step.

She backed around the end of her car, readjusting her direction, until she was backing toward the door to the laundry room. "Marsh," she said again, a rebuke.

And a plea.

When she got to the door, she reached behind her, fumbling for the knob.

He kept coming. He got to her before she got the door open. He raised both hands, cradled her chin in them. The warm pads of his fingers caressed her jawline, slid under her hair. His palms were at her throat.

And a wonderful, naughty weakness was moving through her. She dropped her arm to her side, gave up on trying to get hold of the doorknob.

He whispered into her upturned face, "You could...let me stay with you. Just for tonight. I don't want to go back to that damn hotel, to turn off the lights. And see my father's eyes."

She knew what he meant. Blake Bravo's eyes had been shut at the hospital. She had been very, very glad for that.

Marsh said, ‘‘I'd rather see *your* eyes. Just for tonight.’’

‘‘We don't [illegible] Oh, Marsh. The love we had…we don't have that anymore.’’

‘‘No, we don't,’’ he said. And she almost wished he'd lied, sworn he loved her, that he'd never *stopped* loving her. A lie would have made things easier, a lie really would have helped.

But he didn't lie. He said, ‘‘I want you.’’ He brushed his lips against hers. ‘‘You know that, don't you?’’ She sighed again. He said, ‘‘You seem to want me.’’

‘‘It's wrong…’’

‘‘Just tell me. Do you want me?’’

She shut her eyes. ‘‘I…’’ She could not make the words come.

He put his thumb against her lips, rubbed it maddeningly back and forth. ‘‘Just nod. Or shake your head.’’

She pressed her eyes tighter together. And she did it. Lifted her chin. Lowered it. Whispered, ‘‘Oh, God,’’ against that caressing thumb.

My sin, she was thinking. This man is my sin. All my life I've done right. Been a good girl.

Except for ten years ago, with Marsh.

And now, here he is again.

Different.

But still, I do want him. I want him so much….

His mouth came down on hers again, stealing her

breath away, along with any last shred of will she might have used to resist him.

She sighed some more. And she moaned. His tongue came into her mouth, swept the moist surfaces there, learning them, claiming them for his own.

He moved in closer, pressing his body to hers in a burning brand, laying his right forearm against the door behind her, deepening a kiss she would have sworn could not get any deeper.

She heard a low, rumbling sound. It took her already-overloaded senses a few seconds to realize what that sound was: the far garage door, the one behind his car. He must have pushed the button to shut it. His other arm was by her head now, one arm on either side of her, surrounding her, holding her there.

Not that she wanted to be anywhere else.

"So long," she was thinking. "It's been so long..." She heard the words and realized she had said them aloud.

He groaned in response, and rubbed more strongly against her. She felt his arousal, his body talking to hers. And she felt her body answering, going all hot and wet and needful, getting ready for him.

And then he let go of her mouth. His lips made a sliding kiss, up over her cheek, to her temple, to the side of her head.

He swore. A very bad word. Right into her ear.

"Marsh." She moaned—she couldn't help that, the moaning. "Shame on you."

His mouth was in her hair. She felt his breath, moist. Hot. "I've got nothing. No protection." He pulled back enough to look down at her. His eyes were so dark then. She could fall into them and never get out.

Never *want* to get out.

He said, "If I leave you alone and go take care of this problem, you're going to change your mind, aren't you?"

She only looked at him, catching her lower lip between her teeth and worrying at it a little.

He pressed himself closer, down there, making a taunt of his maleness. "Aren't you?"

She sighed. Changing her mind would be the right thing. The best thing. If she had any sense at all she would make him go looking, send him to the new Wal-Mart Supercenter over on Interstate Drive, which was open 24-7 and would certainly have what he needed. That would give her time to wise up a little.

He looked at her all too knowingly. "By the time I get back, you'll have the bed turned down in your spare room—or you'll make regretful noises and pack me off to my hotel. Won't you?"

She huffed out a breath and gave him a nod. He swore again. Before she could reprimand him for using more bad words, he had captured her mouth and was kissing her deeply, a kiss that sent her spinning back into weakness and heat and pure womanly need.

That particular kiss, however deep, was way too short. Too soon, he was dragging his mouth off hers again, pinning her with those dark, dark eyes. "To hell with it. I'm not leaving. I'll be careful. We'll do everything but."

She could not keep herself from reminding him,

"That's what you used to say. When we were kids. And you know what ended up happening then."

He threw his head back and let out a groan at the ceiling. The garage door light, set on a timer that would give a person long enough to get inside, went out.

He muttered through the darkness, "This is just great."

She supposed he'd suffered enough. "It's all right, Marsh. I have what we need."

He got very still. She could feel him looking at her, though there wasn't enough light to make out his eyes. "You do?"

"Yes. In a drawer in my room. A few years ago I started thinking that it was about time I had myself a little fling."

"A fling?"

"You know, I'm not real thrilled with the way you said that. As if you can't believe someone like me would have such a thing as a fling."

"That's not what I was thinking. Not at all."

"No? Then what?"

He hesitated, muttered, "Never mind." Then he instructed more forcefully, "Go on."

She considered insisting that he tell her what was in his mind on the subject of herself and a fling. But she didn't act on that thought. It would probably only make her irritated with him, ruin the mood, so to speak, to hear whatever he might have to say. And though ruining the mood was a good idea, she had no intention of doing any such thing.

Oh, tonight she *was* bad. A bad girl.

But for some reason, she didn't *feel* bad at all.

She said, "Well, I thought I should go out and have myself a fling. But considering my...past experience, I wanted it to be a *safe* sort of fling—or at least, as safe as a fling can ever be."

"So you bought condoms."

She was glad that he had said the word so she didn't have to. "That's right."

"And you had a fling."

"Well, not exactly. I never got around to the actual fling. A single mom with a business to run has very limited potential for getting herself into the right situation where a fling might be likely to occur."

"No fling?"

"That's right—well, until now. At last, the...opportunity has presented itself. You're here. Kim isn't."

She waited, feeling the blush creep into her cheeks, glad he couldn't see it, hoping he would say something.

But he didn't. His silence seemed thoughtful. She heard herself asking nervously, "This counts, doesn't it, you and me, tonight? As a fling?"

"Is that what you want it to be? A fling?"

"Oh, Marsh. We keep asking each other questions. But neither of us is answering."

He was thoughtful again. Then she felt his lips brush her cheek. He whispered, "Point taken. Maybe we should quit talking."

She lifted her arms and twined them around his neck. His shoulders felt so hard and broad. And that shocked her a little, reminded her all over again of how much he had changed.

A shiver went through her. He must have felt it, with his body so close, touching hers all down the front.

She lifted her face to him and whispered back, "Good idea. No more talking, at least not about flings."

It was all the encouragement he required. His mouth closed over hers and he reached behind her, opened the door.

She didn't need a lot of urging to start walking backward again, stepping up into the laundry room and going on, kissing him hungrily as they went. They paused in the middle of the kitchen, to kiss for a while without the distraction of trying to walk at the same time.

But then he was urging her to get going again. She went on, moving backward, through the kitchen and the family room, into the long central hall and down it.

All the way down.

Chapter Eight

The last door on the left opened onto the master bedroom. Tory had left on the lamp with the teal-colored shade, the one that sat on the high bureau a few feet from her four-poster bed.

"Pretty," Marsh said, still kissing her as they stepped over the threshold. She wasn't sure if he meant the blush-pink walls and the sea-green and rose bed linens—or herself.

Not that it mattered.

She walked backward to the side of the bed and stopped there. They went on kissing. Kissing forever.

His hands moved over her, caressing at the same time as they unbuttoned her buttons and peeled her clothes away. She lost her shirt first and then her slacks. She kicked off her sandals all on her own. He undid the back hook of her bra without her even realizing it—until he was sliding the straps down her arms and taking it away.

He cupped her breasts in those long hands. And her knees went to jelly, at the feel of that, her nipples pressed into his palms. He ran his hands downward, and around to her back, pulling her up against him again, so that the slightly rough fabric of his polo shirt abraded the tender skin of her breasts. But not in a hurting way, oh no. In the most delicious, lovely way....

His hands strayed farther down, over her waist, sliding under the elastic of her panties. He cupped her bottom, pulled her even closer than before.

And still, they kissed. They kissed and kissed.

He took her panties then, sliding them down. She was naked in no time. Naked in his arms.

He broke the endless kiss.

He stepped back.

A sudden shyness bloomed in her. Instinctively she moved to cover herself.

"No. Don't..." It was a plea.

One she couldn't help but grant. She let her arms go lax at her sides and she let him look.

He said, "I never saw you naked..."

And she thought of the two of them, their younger selves, entwined in the back seat of that old Plymouth of his, out at Ten Mile Flat. Of the urgency of their loving, the secretiveness. Of how they never dared to take off all their clothes.

"I never thought..." he began, then seemed not to know how to go on.

She knew. "...that we'd be alone, together, like this, again?"

He nodded. "You're so beautiful, Tory."

You're so beautiful.

She supposed that was probably just one of the things men said when they took a woman to bed. But it didn't matter how many men had said it or how many women had believed it.

She believed it now. And it pleased her mightily. She felt all shivery and fine, her whole body glowing and hungry and...alive.

So very alive.

She stepped forward, put her hands on the sides of his hard waist and gathered his shirt in her fists. She slid it upward. He raised his arms obligingly. She pulled it off and tossed it on the chair by the bureau.

His powerful chest confronted her. She saw the scars, the marks his evil daddy had left on him, faded down to almost nothing by now, small welts and creases that spoke of old hurts. There was one, a thin, white ridge, at the place where his arm joined his shoulder. She pressed her lips to it, causing Marsh to whisper her name in a way that sent a shiver down through her.

To steady herself, she brought up her hands and laid them against his chest, against the mat of crisp dark hair, against the hardness and heat of him. Against the deep, steady beat of his heart.

Next came his belt. It was a very well-made caramel-colored leather belt. She unhooked it and slithered it free of the loops. She tossed it away.

And then she undid his slacks, slid them down. He

wore silk boxers—indigo silk, with a royal-purple waistband.

That surprised her. *Her* Marsh had always worn plain white briefs.

"There is inevitably some awkwardness, at this point." He was standing above her, looking down. She had knelt to slide his slacks off, but there was a problem. His beautiful soft leather shoes were in the way.

She looked up at him, in his silk boxers, with his pants around his ankles. "I see what you mean."

"I think I'd better take it from here."

"Well, you just be my guest."

The straight chair where they'd thrown most of their clothes wasn't far away. He was looking at it significantly. She got the message, rising and scooping up the clothes and carrying them to an easy chair in the sitting area.

When she turned back to him, he had already dropped to the straight chair and was removing those expensive shoes of his. Once he'd dispensed with the shoes, he got rid of his socks. Finally, he could take off the slacks, which he did, rising and draping them over the chair.

He faced her, wearing only those midnight-blue boxer shorts. She remained in the sitting area, next to the pile of their clothes. She was starting to feel a little too naked again.

"Come back here." It was an order. He never used to give her orders. "Please."

That was more like it. She went to him. He reached for her and scooped her up, high in his arms. And then he laid her on the bed.

He stretched out beside her.

She remembered the condoms, tried to sit up. “I'll just get the—”

“Shh,” he said. “Later.”

“But we really have to be careful, Marsh. We can't be foolish and make the same mistake we made before. We have to—”

He kissed her some more.

She forgot all about being careful. His hands moved over her, evoking extraordinary responses, making her feel things she'd all but forgotten she could feel. He took her nipple in his mouth, drawing on it. She clutched his dark head and pulled him closer, cradling him as he suckled her.

He caressed her belly. His hand cupped the side of her waist—and moved down, stroking along the outer curve of her hip.

And then, so slowly, back up again.

She moaned when he buried his fingers in the auburn curls where her thighs joined. And she pressed her legs together in a last, hopeless attempt to shield herself from this endless, incredible invasion of her senses.

He didn't push her. He made a low, soothing sound deep in his throat. And he continued touching her, combing his fingers through the tight auburn strands, then tracing a maddening path, from the base of her belly, around and down, across both her thighs, and up again—making a circle around the place she kept from him.

Finally, with a long moan, she let her thighs fall open. His mouth was on hers again by then. He caught her lower lip between his teeth, bit down lightly, then let go.

His hand found her. She moaned some more as he began caressing her in that most private of places. She was so very wet, so utterly ready. He touched the nub at the heart of her sex, and then slid two fingers inside of her, cupping her, rubbing her with the heel of his hand.

It happened all at once. In a burst of heat and light and shimmering sensation. He kept his hand there, kept on stroking her, as fulfillment shuddered through her.

She buried her face against his hard shoulder. He gathered her close. For a little while they simply lay there, all wrapped up together as she gradually came back to herself.

"All right," he whispered. He stroked her hair, tipped her chin up to make her look at him. "Now you can tell me. Where are they?"

She was thinking again how changed he was. And that there must have been other women, a number of them, because he certainly did seem to know what a woman liked.

He had been very dear all those years ago. But he had also been every bit as inexperienced as she. There had been a lot of fumbling, on both of their parts.

He didn't seem to fumble much now.

He kissed her nose. "You are looking serious. Maybe too serious."

"You asked me. But I didn't ask you. I know you never married. But maybe there's someone…waiting for you. In Chicago."

''Is that a question?''

''Yes. Yes, it is.''

He tipped her chin higher. ''Tory, there's no one *waiting*, as you put it. If there were, I wouldn't be here, in this bed. With you.''

''Well. That's good to hear.''

''You mean, that I'm not cheating on anyone?''

''Yes.''

''I'm not a cheater. I thought you knew that.''

''I did. It's only that so much has changed.''

''I haven't changed—not about that, at least.''

''I am glad.''

He pulled her close again, snuggled her head into his shoulder. He stroked her hair some more.

After a few minutes she got up and got the box of condoms from way in the back of a bureau drawer. She set them on the nightstand near at hand and then lay down beside him again. She kissed him.

And he kissed her. On her mouth—and lower, down her neck, between her breasts. She put up not even token resistance, when he lowered his head between her thighs. With a needful cry, she clutched his broad shoulders and spread her legs wider.

Just before she reached the peak again, he rose up above her. He was swift, adept, at getting the condom out of the box, free of its wrapping and into place.

She watched him, thinking that once she had known him right down to the center of himself—that some part of her felt she knew him still.

And yet, at the same time, she didn't know him at all.

It seemed so right, the two of them, here. In her bed, taking up where they'd left off a decade ago.

So right.

And completely insane.

And for tonight, she might as well concentrate on the rightness, since they *were* doing this, would probably keep on doing this, until tonight became tomorrow.

He slid into her easily. Her body gave him no resistance. As if it recognized him, welcomed him, at last, after so long.

He lay over her, pressing her down, and she wrapped her arms and legs around him, pushing herself up to him, meeting each thrust. He threw his head back when completion claimed him. And he pushed in so hard and deep that she found her own fulfillment spinning into being, out of his.

Her cry was his cry. It was all one.

Around 3:00 a.m., Marsh woke.

He saw that everything had really happened. Tory was here. In bed with him—or maybe he should say, *he* was here, in *her* bed.

His wicked old dad had died.

And he had a little girl, Kimberly Marsha, who had dark eyes and brown hair, a fine collection of small stuffed animals called Beanie Babies, and who sometimes got Bs in math.

Tory lay on her back, her face turned away from him, a corkscrew curl of silky red hair trailing across her white throat. He turned on his side, toward her. And he put his finger, very gently, against that red curl. He guided it off her throat and smoothed it out, with the rest of her hair, on the pale-green pillow.

She woke. He watched the red lashes flutter open, heard her small sigh, waited for her to turn to him.

She did, meeting his eyes, whispering his name.

He was hard again. Just like that, with wanting her.

He curled his hand around her nape, spearing his fingers up into the warm red fall of her hair. And he brought his mouth down onto hers, drinking her sweetness. She responded by pressing closer to him, reaching up to wrap her arms around him. They shared one of those kisses that never seemed to end. He touched her, running his hand down her body, until he found the female heart of her.

Wet.

Ready.

He reached for the box on the bedside again, and when that was taken care of, he pulled her over on top of him. The red hair fell, living fire, against her slim, pale shoulders. She looked down at him as she lowered herself onto him. She rode him, a slow, rocking ride, holding his eyes all the while as they moved together.

But she couldn't keep that lazy pace. Not indefinitely.

And he could not have taken it if she had.

She moved faster. He surged up to meet her, pulling her down, so that he could have her mouth again. He kissed her as his climax rolled through him, lifting him up and emptying him out. She bucked frantically against him and then she gave a long, low cry.

He held her close, pressed his mouth to her throat,

right under the curve of her jaw. He could feel the beat of her heart there, against his lips. He put out his tongue, tasted the sweet and salt of her skin…

Tory heard birds singing outside.

She pushed her mind up through the layers of sleep, awareness dawning as she woke.

She was in her own bed. And Marsh was here with her. She lay on her side, facing the edge of the bed. She couldn't see him. But she could feel him, close at her back, his leg just touching hers. She could hear his breathing—even, shallow and slow.

The bedroom was dark. That last time they woke, after they made love again, she had risen and turned off the lamp. But the clock on the bedside table said it would be dawn very soon. She could not afford to drift back to sleep again.

Her stomach went all fluttery as she recalled the sinful things they'd done. Carefully, so as not to wake him until she was ready to meet his eyes, she turned to him.

He lay on his side, his shadowed face stern in sleep. She wanted to reach up a hand, trace the shape of his brow, touch his eyelids and the silky long lashes. To run her finger down that blade of a nose, to feel his mouth, his breath flowing down her fingers into her palm.

But she kept her hand to herself, her mind skipping away from tender thoughts of caressing him, focusing on what had to be done right now.

Rayanne Pickett was an early riser. She didn't want

Rayanne deciding to bring Kim home before she got Marsh out of the house.

I must wake him, ask him to go....

Once he left, she would shower, get dressed, collect her daughter from next door. And then...

Well, Marsh had the arrangements for his father to worry about. Even if there would be no funeral, he would have to visit the funeral home, get everything set up with them for the cremation. And he'd probably want to go out to his father's house and make sure all was in order there. And she had to get Kimmy off to school and get over to the shop by nine.

Kimmy.

Thinking of Kim brought apprehension, a tightness in her chest and in her stomach.

Maybe later, maybe that night, the two of them would talk, would come to some sort of agreement about Kim.

What would he want, when it came to Kim?

Her mind skittered away from that question—and why shouldn't it? There was no way to know what he'd want, anyway, until they talked it all out.

She stared at his sleeping face some more, at his strong neck and deep chest. She looked at his hand lying on the coverlet. And she felt that little curl of excitement, of yearning, down inside herself.

Well, there was no doubt about it. She was still just completely gone on him, at least in the physical sense. Even now, after spending a whole night doing things she probably shouldn't have let herself do, even now, when she needed to get him up and out of here, even now...

She couldn't stop thinking about reaching out and touching his face, about running her hand down his throat, over his shoulder, along that muscular arm....

Well, all right. So she was gone on him.

And was that it? Was that *all* of it, just this powerful yearning, this thing called desire?

Or could it be that what she felt was more? That her love for him, in spite of years of constant effort to convince herself otherwise, had never died, that—

Oh, it was all too confusing. She couldn't possibly figure it out right now.

She wanted him. She knew that much.

Too bad she had also learned the hard way that wanting and having did not always add up to the same thing.

He opened his eyes. They gleamed at her through the dimness, fully alert. She wondered if he'd really been sleeping at all.

She gave him a smile that she tried to make bright. "It's almost daylight. We have to—"

He cut her off. He did it with a look, his eyes going soft, heavy with the promise of sensual delights.

"Marsh. I mean it. We have no more time for—"

He hooked his hand around her neck and pulled her close—so close that you could have barely slipped a feather between his mouth and hers. "We have time. Kiss me."

"Have you noticed—" she strove for firmness "—that you have become a person who interrupts a lot?"

"I like to think of it as cutting to the chase."

"Call it what you want. We have to—"

"We will. Soon. But right now kiss me."

"Marsh. You are not listening to me."

"That's right, I'm not. Kiss me."

Well, what could she do? With that wonderful mouth of his so close, tempting her like that?

She kissed him.

So much for getting right up and getting him out of there.

She kissed him, and he put those magical hands of his on her body, his fingers opening her, delving in, stroking until she was moaning and crying out, forgetting all about Rayanne Pickett and Kimmy and all the things she and Marsh needed to be saying to each other, all the things that would so change their lives....

Soon enough she was reaching for the condom herself, tearing the package open, rolling the thing down over him.

And then he was inside her and she was past forgetting, past caring about anything but the feel of him, the magic between them that had somehow survived, still fresh and new, after all this time. They moved together, frantic and needful, slowly and so very deliciously.

It didn't last long enough. Too soon her climax was pulsing through her, and she was clutching him tight against her as he found his own release.

At the end he eased himself to the side, turning her with him, so they remained joined, facing each other, her thigh draped over his hip. She kissed him and sighed and wished they could just stay there, forever, in bed.

He echoed her thoughts. "I don't want to move.

Ever. Except eventually to make love to you some more.''

She sighed again.

He chuckled. ''I know what these sighs you're giving me now mean.''

''Oh, and what is that?''

''I'm not going to get what I want.''

She made a soft sound, one with a clear note of regret in it. ''You have to go, and we both know it.''

He crooked a finger under her chin, lifting it so he could kiss the tip of her nose. ''We have a lot to say to each other.''

''We will. I promise. Tonight.''

His eyes searched hers, as if he doubted the truth of her promise. And then he shrugged. ''Tonight, then.'' He pressed his mouth to hers once more, but quickly, a man reconciled to going.

And then he was pulling away. She found she missed him already, though he hadn't even left the bed.

He rolled to his other side to get up—and then he froze.

He swore, low and with feeling.

She canted up on an elbow. ''What?''

He looked over his shoulder at her. He didn't say anything. There was no need. She could see for herself.

The condom had broken.

Chapter Nine

He was glaring at her. ''How old *are* these damn things?''

''Marsh—''

''Just answer me. How old?''

She did not like his accusing tone, not one bit. ''I *told* you last night. A few years.''

''A few years.'' He swore again. ''What is the date on them?''

She picked up the box, found the date stamped on the side. ''Well,'' she said, wishing she could just fall through the floor. ''The news is not good.''

''Say it.''

''The date already went by—but only just barely.''

He took the box from her, read the date, swore again. ''We should have checked the damn date.''

Like she needed to hear that now. "Yes, we should have. But we didn't, did we?"

"And what brand is this? I've never even heard of it."

"Is that some kind of an accusation?"

"These things are usually the next thing to indestructible. Damn it, Tory. A condom is not something you should try to get a bargain on."

"I didn't. I'm sorry. I'm no expert on those things."

He made a low, disgusted noise in his throat. "I do not believe this." Then he left her, just swung his legs off the bed and stalked toward her bathroom. She heard the toilet flush and then water running in the sink.

Seconds later, he was back. He flicked on a lamp and snatched up his boxer shorts. He shoved his legs into them. Then he went to the pile of clothes on the easy chair and untangled his pants and his shirt from them. He pulled on the clothes.

She sat in the bed, hugging the covers, counting the days since her last period.

Not good. Not good at all.

He came back to the small chair by the bureau, grabbed his belt and put it on. Then he dropped into the chair and shoved his feet into his shoes and his socks.

Fully dressed, though slightly rumpled and clearly in need of a shave, he stood again. He regarded her through eyes she found impossible to read. "You look terrified."

She made herself shrug. "Well, I'm not. I mean, come on. What are the odds that it could happen again with us?'' She expected him to reassure her that the odds were very slim.

Apparently, he was not in a reassuring frame of mind. ''We've already proven once that it *can* happen with us. So now it's probably just a question of whether or not it's the time of the month when you're likely to get pregnant.''

She cut her eyes away, which, of course, told him everything he needed to know. Outside she could hear a mocker squawking. But inside, the silence was truly deafening.

He broke it by swearing some more. ''It's the right time of the month for you, isn't it?''

She still wouldn't look at him. But she did admit, ''It's the time when I should be the most careful, yes.''

He muttered something under his breath—no doubt more swear words. ''What a damn mess.''

She yanked her sagging shoulders up straight. ''Oh, stop it. There's no point in getting all stirred up about this right now. Most likely nothing will come of it.''

He grunted. ''I'm sure we tried to tell each other the same thing all those years ago, after we did what we said we weren't going to do.'' He frowned. ''Didn't we?''

She found she had no desire to answer that question, so she fiddled with the covers instead, arranging them more modestly around herself.

But he wouldn't let her off the hook. He dropped down beside her on the bed and leaned in way too close. ''Didn't we?''

She gave the sheet a last irritated tug. ''As a matter of fact, yes, we did. The three times it happened, we talked about how it hadn't happened often and we were both sure people hardly ever got pregnant after only a time or two."

"Right. And have you noticed that telling ourselves you weren't going to get pregnant did *not* stop it from happening?"

"Well, just because I got pregnant then doesn't mean it will necessarily be the same now."

"Denial is not a river in Egypt."

"Is that supposed to be a joke?"

"I promise you, Tory. I'm deadly serious."

He was still glaring at her. He looked angry and frustrated, and she hated that his looking like that made her feel guilty. As if what had happened was all her fault.

Well, all right. It *was* her fault. But it was *his* fault, too.

And what did it matter *whose* fault it was? They might or might not end up with another baby on the way. But there was no way to know if they would right at the moment, so what was the point of worrying about it now?

She slid a glance at the clock. Six a.m. She could definitely see light through the crack in the curtains.

"Marsh. We really don't have time to go into all this now."

He glared all the harder. "You're always evading. In the past thirty-six hours you've put me off about ten times."

She clutched the sheet closer. "I can see you have picked up a tendency to exaggerate along with all the other ways that you have changed."

He folded his arms across his chest. ''I'm not leaving until we work a few things out.''

''I told you, now is not the time.''

''Have you noticed that since I came back, it's never the time? You've always got some excuse why we can't tackle any tough questions right now.''

''You keep *blaming* me.''

''I don't.''

''You do—and maybe I am to blame. But I'm not the only one at fault. I was willing to talk last night. It was not my fault that the hospital called. And then later I invited you back here to the house with me. I made coffee. You had another chance then, for talking, if you'd wanted to take it. But you didn't say anything. You drank your coffee and said you had to go. You *would* have gone—but then I made the mistake of asking you if there was anything I could do, to please let me know. And you came up with kissing. And just look where that has gotten us.''

He must have seen the truth in what she said. He unfolded his arms and spoke in a gentler tone. ''Listen. I don't want to blame you. I just want to talk. It's barely six. Do you really expect me to believe that Rayanne Pickett will be knocking on the door in the next fifteen or twenty minutes?''

He had a point there. She was forced to confess, ''No. Rayanne will probably call about seven—that is, if I don't call her first.''

''So can you spare me a few minutes?''

She just looked at him, thinking that in spite of her own very reasonable arguments to the contrary, he was right: she was such a coward. She didn't really want to tackle all these problems they were facing.

"Tory," he said gently. "Please."

"Yes. All right." She tugged on the sheet again, accomplishing nothing because he was sitting on the covers and holding them where they were. "But I mean it. By six-thirty at the latest, you have to go. Maybe it's cowardly of me, maybe I should be a bigger, braver person, but I do not want to explain to Rayanne or to our daughter what you were doing here all night. I do not want to have to decide whether or not to lie and pretend that you stayed in the spare room."

He arched an eyebrow. "You know, it's highly likely that someone is going to see me pulling out of your garage, anyway."

"I can't do anything about that. But I *can* make sure nobody catches you here in my bedroom."

"All right. I understand. Now can we stop wasting time on the possibility of getting 'caught,' as you put it? Can we get back to what we're going to do about Kim—and the baby we just might have made a few minutes ago?"

She wanted to scoff some more, wanted to argue with him, to convince him—and herself, as well—that she couldn't possibly be pregnant again. But she held her tongue. She could scoff all she wanted, it wouldn't change the truth—whatever the truth ultimately turned out to be.

He spoke again. "Marry me."

He said it in a bland, unemotional sort of way, the

way a man will say "Pass the salt," or "Let's have those string beans down here."

Tory's first reaction was that she must not have heard right. "Uh, excuse me?"

"I said, marry me. And stop looking at me as if I've just asked you to jump off a cliff."

"I'm not." Well, maybe she was. But she thought it prudent not to admit it. "I just...you surprised me, that's all."

"It's the best way to go. We're both unattached. We have a daughter together and there may be another baby on the way. We're still attracted to each other." He paused, gave her a long look, then asked, "What do you think?"

Think?

He expected her to *think?* Her heart had kicked into high gear. It was racing way too fast. And her face was much too warm.

Marsh had asked her to marry him.

After all these years.

Her most cherished dream at last coming true.

Except that in her old, vanished dream he would speak at length on the subject of how very much he loved her. He would say he'd come back because he couldn't forget her. That he longed only for a life at her side.

The reality wasn't stacking up to be quite so romantic. His proposal, to put it kindly, had come out lacking in sentiment.

And he had not come back because he couldn't forget her.

It had been the obligation he felt to a dying man

that had finally brought him home. And he was proposing now because he felt an obligation to her, as the mother of his child. And to that child herself, to Kim. And most of all, it seemed, to the baby that probably wasn't—but *could* be.

He must have realized that his proposal had suffered from a certain shortage of feeling. He leaned closer and he spoke in that low, intimate tone that reminded her of how wonderful it felt—still, after all these years—whenever he touched her. "We loved each other once. And the...chemistry is still there. Who's to say we can't learn to love each other again?"

We loved each other once. Past tense.

How terribly sad.

She tried to focus on the tempting low sweetness of his voice, to tell herself that he wasn't saying anything she didn't already know. He'd made it very clear last night that he didn't love her anymore. And he was making it clear now that he thought maybe he *could* come to love her again—and that was all to the good.

The question entered her mind, as it had earlier, when she lay in this bed beside him, thinking she had to wake him and rush him out of the house.

Did *she* still love *him?*

And if she did, then who, really, did she love? The troubled boy who had held her heart in his trembling hands was no more. This man *was* a stranger, in so many ways.

He said, "I can provide a good life for you now. You and Kim will have the best of everything. I can see to that."

She folded her hands and looked down at them,

studying them as if there might be something new about them.

He had moved on from talk of love pretty quickly. And maybe he had it right. Maybe it would be better to leave love out of it, for the time being. To think about this logically.

Logic told her that there would be some real benefits to accepting his proposal.

If she married him, the custody issue wouldn't even have to come up. They'd all live together. And Kim would have *her* dream. They'd be a family—with, just possibly, that little sister she'd always wanted coming along in nine months.

And *where* would they live?

Tory had a sinking feeling she knew the answer to that without even asking. She slanted him a glance. "You'd want us to move to Chicago, wouldn't you?"

He let out a long breath. "Tory, that's where my company is."

"Would you answer my question, please? Would you want us to move to Chicago and live with you there?"

He took a long time to reply. But when he spoke, he said just what she'd expected he would. "Yes, that's what I would want."

She glanced down at her hands again, then made herself look back up at him. "I have to have a little time. To think this over."

He smiled then, a rueful sort of smile. "Sure. It's 6:10. Take twenty minutes."

"I was thinking more along the lines of a few days."

"A few days." He didn't look very happy about that.

"Marsh, it's a big decision."

He was silent. But then finally he asked, "What will we tell Kim, in the meantime?"

"We'll tell her the truth—at least, a simplified version of it."

"That I asked you to marry me and you're considering it?"

She shook her head. "That's a little more truth than I had in mind. She'd be completely crushed if it didn't work out."

"We both know how to keep that from happening. Say yes now."

She gave him a pained look.

He gave her a scowl in return. "Then what?"

"We'll say that you're...staying in town for a few days, and we're all going to spend a lot of time together, get to know each other, get to see if it might work out for the three of us to be together *all* of the time."

He kept on scowling. "I've known my daughter less than twenty-four hours and I can already guess what she'll say to that."

So could Tory. "Okay. She won't be too thrilled about it. She wants us to get married, and in her mind, she's already picked out her maid-of-honor dress. But you told her yourself—she is not the one to make this decision."

"No," he said, rather coldly. "*You* are."

She shook her head. "*We* are. And I think we have

a responsibility to be certain it's the *right* decision, for all of us.''

''How long do you need, to be certain?''

Did he really expect her to be able to answer such a question right then? Judging by the grim set to his jaw and the hard light in his eyes, he certainly did.

''How long?'' he asked again.

''Marsh, we can't just—''

''How long?''

''Please try to understand how I feel. I've lived in Norman all my life. Everybody I know is here. My shop is here. You're asking me to just...walk away from everything I know—everything our daughter knows. With you.''

''Once you swore that was all you wanted. To walk away from this town—with me.''

''Oh, why do you keep bringing up what happened way back when? I was sixteen and we were crazy in love. You thought you had killed that father of yours and you were desperate to get away. *I* didn't want to get away. *I* just wanted to be with you.''

''And now I'm offering you what you said you wanted.''

''You're a few years too late, and you know it. And what I'm trying to tell you is, that situation was nothing like this one.''

''No, it wasn't. Now I have a life to offer you. Now we have a daughter together. Now we just might have another—''

''Wait. That's enough of that. I think we need to stop talking about what *might* be and think about what *is.*''

He leaned in to her again, so close she felt his warm breath on her face, so close that the pull of attraction between them seemed a magnetic force, charging the air around them. "What might be *is* what matters. You had my baby once without me. I hate that it happened that way. I'm not going to let it happen that way again. Damn it, I *will* be what I never had—a good father. If you're pregnant, you will marry me."

Tory realized that her mouth was hanging open. She clamped it shut.

The independent, self-directed woman she'd been forced to become wanted to tell him he could take this new, overbearing side of himself and put it where the sun refused to shine.

But where would that get them?

If she *were* pregnant, she would want to keep her baby. And she did believe in certain values. She believed in the power of love. And in the sanctity and importance of the family, in a man and a woman binding their lives together, committing themselves to each other and to working together to make a good future for themselves and their children. Though she had had Kim without the benefit of marriage, she really didn't want to do the same thing all over again if she could possibly avoid it.

If there *was* another baby coming, she would say yes to Marsh in a New York minute. She'd pack up herself and Kimmy and move to Chicago with him. She'd put her whole heart and soul into making their marriage work.

Truly, the more she thought about it, the more it seemed clear that the possibility of another baby was the real reason they were having this discussion. Marsh hadn't so much as hinted at the idea of marriage until that darned condom had given way.

And if, just for a minute here, she could keep all the confusion of her own feelings out of it, if she could look at the situation through his eyes....

How had he said it just now? *I* will *be what I never had—a good father.*

He had missed his daughter's birth and the first nine years of her life. No matter how much he wanted to be with Kim, now that he'd found her, reality had to be telling him that his newfound daughter had a good life established here in Norman. She had her friends and her school and a fine home—the only home she'd ever known. Kim could demand that he marry her mother and start playing full-time father all she wanted. Kim was nine, she didn't think ahead, would not even consider what it would be like, starting over in a strange new place. But Marsh could think ahead. He could see the same consequences Tory could. There would be difficulties in uprooting Kim.

A new baby, however, would be something else altogether.

A new baby would be like a fresh start. A chance to do the right thing and do it well.

A chance, as Marsh had just said himself, to *be* the father he'd never had....

"What are you thinking?" His tone defined the word *suspicious.*

"All right," she said.

He sat back, looked at her sideways. "All right, what?"

‘‘If it turns out there *is* a baby coming, I will marry you.’’

‘‘If?’’

‘‘Yes. If. We’ll wait. A couple of weeks, until my monthly time. And if it doesn’t come on schedule, I’ll take one of those home tests. If it turns out I am going to have another baby, we’ll get married.’’

His expression said he found her suggestion thoroughly ridiculous. ‘‘Wait two weeks?’’

‘‘Yes, Marsh. A home test gives a result you can depend on as soon as a woman turns up late. I’m usually very…regular. And I am due in two weeks.’’

‘‘You’re an expert on home pregnancy tests?’’

‘‘Oh, stop looking at me like that. One of my clerks has a daughter and the daughter and her husband have been trying to have a baby. I hear a lot about things like home tests and when’s the best time to—’’

‘‘Never mind. I get the picture. And I’m sorry. I don’t think I’m following this. Just a minute ago you said you’d give me an answer in a few days. Now it’s suddenly going to take you two weeks.’’

‘‘No, I’m giving you my answer right now. Yes, if I’m pregnant. No, if I’m not.’’

He looked so much like his daughter right then—his daughter when she’d heard something she didn’t want to hear.

She suggested, carefully, ‘‘It *is* the baby—I mean, the chance that there might be one. That’s what this is all about, isn’t it?’’

‘‘Yeah. So?’’

‘‘So we’ll wait. To see if there *is* a baby. Then we’ll go on from there. And while we’re waiting, well, whatever time you can manage to spend here, in Norman, would be just great. We can all be together, as much as possible. You and I can get to know each other again. And you and Kim can start to...build a relationship.''

She expected more arguments. But he surprised her. He asked, ''You mean...I would stay here, in this house, with you and Kim?''

She said, ''Yes,'' automatically. Of course he should stay here.

But then Rayanne Pickett's face flashed through her mind—Rayanne's face wearing a disapproving expression. She qualified, ''In the spare room, I mean. I think that's the best way to go.'' Rayanne wouldn't approve of him staying in the house at all. But that was Rayanne's problem. Tory did want a chance for them to grow closer, and having him in the house would make that all the more likely. Yes, people might talk. But people had talked ten years ago and she'd lived to hold her head up high.

''You're serious,'' he said. ''You're agreeing that I can stay here, in your house.'' He said each word carefully, as if the whole idea was something outlandish and incomprehensible to him. ''In the spare room...''

''Yes.''

A silence ensued. A long one. Then he gave out grudgingly, ''I might be willing to do that.''

''Good.''

''But I'd rather sleep with you.'' It was a simple statement of fact, one that sent a naughty shiver of excitement skimming down her spine.

Unfortunately, they had a child to consider. ''How would you explain *that* to Kim?''

''Who says I'd have to explain it to her?''

''Take my word for it. You'd have to. She would keep after you until you told her something by way of explanation, I guarantee it—probably something you'd live to regret.''

''Kim is a child. Some things are just none of her business.''

''Marsh. Even if you get lucky and she never brings it up, you will be giving your daughter the message that it's okay for people who aren't married to sleep together.''

''Is that so terrible?''

''She's nine years old. I don't think she needs to be getting that kind of message at this point in her life.''

He shrugged. ''I'd say it's a message she'll get one way or the other. How could she help it? She's here—and you and I are not married and never have been.''

''*That* we can write off to being young and foolish and terribly in love. What's our excuse now?''

He steered clear of answering that question and went back to his original argument. ''It's just none of her business what we do behind closed doors.''

''Children learn what they live, Marsh. That's all I'm saying.''

He gave her a long look, a look with weariness in it, a look that said she had finally worn him down. ''All right. The spare room—and I have your agreement. You'll marry me when you find out you're pregnant.''

She almost corrected him: I said *if,* not *when.* But what did it matter? They'd know in a couple of weeks.

And in the meantime they could find out so much more. They'd have a chance to learn about each other, to see if they might be able to become the family Kim had always dreamed of.

It was a good plan, a plan that made the most of a difficult situation.

"Do I have your agreement, Tory?" He sounded very stern.

She gave him a big smile. "Absolutely. If it turns out I'm pregnant, we'll get married."

"And you and Kim will move to Chicago."

"Yes."

"All right, then." He looked relieved more than anything. He added hopefully, "Starting today?"

She dared to reach out, to lay her hand along his beard-shadowed cheek. It felt so good just to touch him.

A little quiver of longing moved through her. She had to admit it, at least to herself. It was going to be tough, being in the same house together and standing firm on the issue of sleeping in separate rooms.

But it was the best way, the wisest way. They needed time to discover other commonalities, and also to see the places they rubbed each other wrong. Really, she felt quite pleased with herself. This *was* a good plan.

He took her hand, opened the fingers, placed a kiss in the heart of her palm. "Well? Does this... arrangement begin today?"

She didn't even hesitate. "There's an extra house

key in that milk-glass bowl on the dresser. And there's a spare garage remote on that shelf right by the laundry room door. Take them both with you and get your things from that hotel.''

Chapter Ten

At his hotel Marsh showered and shaved and put on clean clothes. Then, after spending a few minutes dealing with the automatic checkout on the television in his suite, he carried his suitcases down to the car.

It was just seven-thirty when he pulled out of the hotel's parking lot. He drove straight back to Tory's. Maybe it would have been more considerate to let her and Kim get through their morning routine, to wait to move in on them until the evening, when they wouldn't be rushing around trying to get ready for school and for work.

But to hell with consideration.

Tory had said he could stay with them. She had said "Get your things from that hotel." And that was just what he was doing.

Kim came shooting out of the laundry room as he

pulled into the spare space in the garage. She had a wide smile on that sweet little pixie face of hers. He barely got out of the car before she was climbing all over him. He picked her up and hugged her and felt her small hands patting his back.

When he set her down again, she started talking. "Daddy. Mama said you were coming, that you would be staying here, in our house, for two weeks, except for the times you have to go back to Chicago. She said that it's a *visit* we're having, that we will get to know each other better. I said, 'Does that mean you're getting married after you get to know each other better?' She said, 'We'll see.' I asked again, about the getting-married part. I asked more than once. But she kept saying, 'We'll see,' and I couldn't get her to say anything else about it. So. Daddy. *Are* you getting married when the visit is over?"

He knelt and looked into her face. A miracle, that face. Open and friendly. With gorgeous dimples tucking themselves into her cheeks when she smiled.

"Daddy? Are you going to answer my question?"

He grinned at her. "We'll see."

She groaned. "No fair..."

He took her hand and stood. "Come on. I could use some help here." He led her to the rear of the car and raised the trunk lid, pulling out his laptop first and handing it to Kim. "Be careful with that."

"It's a computer?"

"That's right. Take this, too."

"That's called a briefcase, right—for important papers?"

"Right."

She took the briefcase in her free hand. He reached for his garment bag and grabbed the suitcase underneath it, too. He was giving the trunk lid a shove to close it when Kim stopped him.

"What about that bag there? Don't you need it?"

It was the white plastic bag from the hospital, the one that contained his father's things. "No. I don't need that one."

He half expected her to ask him what was in the bag, but she was already turning to go inside. He shut the trunk and followed her in, thinking that he and Tory *would* have to find some simple, direct way to tell her a little about Blake. It didn't escape him that his father's death made the job a lot easier. Now Marsh wouldn't have to confront the prospect of Kim wanting to meet the old man.

Damn. What a pitiful state of affairs. Here he was, hesitating to introduce his daughter to her grandfather for fear that the pure evilness of the man might have an adverse effect on the child.

Inside, Tory was at the stove, cracking eggs in a bowl. "Scrambled all right?"

She wore a sleeveless knit dress in a cool mint-green color. The dress skimmed all the curves he'd caressed the night before. He wanted to lift the cascade of red curls off her neck and place a kiss there, to breathe in the sweet scent of her, all fresh from her morning shower.

"Scrambled is terrific."

He went and put his stuff in the spare room, Kim dancing ahead of him down the hall, happy as a kitten with a catnip toy. When they returned to the kitchen,

Tory put the eggs in front of him—along with coffee and bacon and biscuits.

"This looks great." And it did. He spooned sugar into the coffee, stirred it. "But what about you two?"

"We ate already. Now I've got to get Kim's lunch together. She has to be out of here in five minutes or less."

While he got to work on the food, Kim babbled away at him about all the things they would do together in the next two weeks. Tory bustled around at the counter, packing a lunch in a bright-yellow insulated bag.

"Soccer practice is tonight at six o'clock," Kim informed him. "You don't have to go to that. Alicia's mom drops us off and Mama picks us up at seven. But parents always go to the games. The games are down at Griffin Park and there's one this Saturday and one more the Saturday after that and then the season will be over—well, except for the big tournament. That will be on Saturday, too—a week *after* the last game. If we win, we will also play on Sunday that week. You don't have to go to Chicago on Saturdays, do you?"

Marsh swallowed a bite of egg. It was fluffy but still moist. Just the way he liked it. "I'll make a point to be here for your games."

"Good. And today, when I come home from school, you can take care of me, and I won't even have to go to Rayanne's. I will—"

"Hold it," said Tory, looking up from sliding a sandwich into the lunch bag. "Marsh and I haven't had a chance to discuss after-school yet. This afternoon you go to Rayanne's.''

Marsh sipped from his coffee mug. ''It's all right. I can be here when she gets home.''

Tory frowned. ''I wasn't sure for today. I already got things up with Rayanne.''

''You can just call her,'' Kim wheedled. ''Tell her my Daddy will take care of me.''

''But I—''

''*Please*, Mama...''

Tory worried her lower lip, then shrugged. ''All right—if you're sure that will work for you, Marsh.''

''No problem.''

''Kim gets home from school at a little before three.''

''I remember.'' He thought of the day before. Damn. Had it only been yesterday that he'd first seen her, running up the front walk? ''If I go out, I'll be back by two-thirty at the latest.''

''That will work fine.''

''Good.'' Kim heaved a big sigh. ''So I'll come straight home. And we can maybe play some more U-No. You will get better at it, if you play it real often. Then comes tonight. There's soccer practice. I already told you about that. And Mom will make dinner, after practice. And I might need some more help on my math. You can do the flash cards with me on my timetables. I always need someone to help me with that. And I also need to—''

''Kim.'' Tory broke through the flood of words. She held out the yellow lunch bag. ''Ten to eight. Better get going or you'll be late.''

The doorbell rang. "That's my best friends." Kim grabbed the lunch bag from Tory. "'Bye, Mom, 'bye, Dad." She flew through the sitting area, pausing only to grab the full-to-bursting purple backpack that leaned at the foot of the easy chair. Seconds later Marsh heard the front door open, a chorus of childish voices, then the door shutting again.

All of a sudden the kitchen seemed very quiet. Marsh glanced at Tory, on the other side of the counter, and caught her staring at him. They both looked away at the same time.

Tory said, "I guess I'd better call Rayanne." She picked up the phone on the wall and punched one of the auto-dial buttons.

Marsh took his attention back to his meal, finishing up that last crispy slice of bacon, splitting a second biscuit and squirting the halves with honey from a squeeze bottle, kind of pretending that he wasn't listening.

But she was only a few feet away. He heard it all.

"Hi, Rayanne. It's Tory. Listen, about this afternoon. It turns out that Marsh is going to look after Kim, so you don't need to worry about her. She'll be—"

Rayanne must have started talking. Tory listened, tipping her head to the side, worrying her lip again.

"Yes," Tory said after a minute, her voice managing to be both cautious and cheerful at the same time. "He's staying here, with Kim and me, for a couple of weeks."

Rayanne said something else.

Tory was fiddling with the phone cord. "That's right. Here. At the house."

Marsh waited for her to add, with emphasis, *In the spare room.* But she didn't, which pleased him in a grim sort of way.

Tory listened some more, then spoke up again. "Well, we need a little time. After all these years. To get to know each other some. So that's what we are going to do. And I just wanted you to know that you don't have to watch Kim today, that Marsh will take care of it.... Yes... Mmm-hmm...I do appreciate your taking her last night.... I know, we really couldn't talk about it earlier, with Kim there.... What?... Oh. No, I'm afraid he didn't make it...."

It took Marsh a second or two to figure out that she meant the old man. By then she was talking again. "No, I don't think that's necessary. There's not going to be any funeral. He didn't want one, evidently... Cremation... That's right... We haven't talked to Kim about him yet, so better just not mention him to her for now. I'll let you know what we tell her. And now I really have to get myself over to the shop.... All right, I will.... You, too. 'Bye."

She hung up and then remained very still for a moment, her hand on the receiver, staring at the wall. At last she turned to him and manufactured a bright smile. "It's all taken care of."

He knew he shouldn't ask, but he did it, anyway. "What did she say?"

"She was...very nice."

Irritation prickled through him. What the hell did that mean? He picked up the paper napkin he'd laid across his thigh and wiped his hands. "Fine. So what did she *say?*"

"Nothing. Really."

"So that was dead air you were talking to?"

A frown etched itself between her brows. "Of course not."

"She freaked, didn't she? At the idea that you have—how did they always used to put it? That Troubled Bravo Boy. Yeah, that's it. She started in on you because you have That Troubled Bravo Boy staying in your house."

"She most certainly did not. She was polite and she didn't say anything the least out of line."

"Everything was in the tone of voice, you mean? In the significant pauses?"

He knew he'd hit home there—because she didn't fall all over herself coming up with denials. In fact, she let what he'd said pass without comment, turning for a moment to glance out the window over the sink.

She looked at him again. "Rayanne did ask about your father."

He shrugged. He'd gathered that from hearing her end of the conversation.

"She wanted to send flowers."

That gave him pause. "She did?"

Tory nodded. "She wanted me to put together a nice bouquet for her, for the funeral. I told her—well, you must have heard what I said. That flowers wouldn't be necessary."

He was still stuck on the idea of Rayanne offering the flowers in the first place. It *was* a kind gesture, especially considering that Rayanne Pickett had never approved of Marsh and hadn't known his evil daddy from Adam. Of course, if she *had* known Blake, the thought of sending flowers for his funeral would have been the last thing to enter her mind. You didn't send flowers in memory of someone like Blake Bravo. He didn't deserve them and he wouldn't have wanted them.

"See?" Tory's blue eyes had taken on a self-satisfied gleam. "Rayanne is a caring woman at heart."

"I never said she wasn't. I just said she doesn't like the idea of my staying in your house."

"Well, she'll just have to get used to it. Because you *are* staying, aren't you?"

"Yes," he said. They shared a long look. "I am."

"There's an empty dresser in the spare room," Tory said a few minutes later. "You can put your things away, if you want to. And I saw Kim bring in that laptop and a briefcase. There's a desk in there, did you notice? Might come in handy, if you need to get some work done. And there are lots of fresh towels, in the lower cabinets in the hall bathroom. And please, help yourself to anything in the refrigerator...."

He thanked her, promised to take full advantage of everything she had offered. He'd finished his meal by then and stood in the kitchen with her, sipping a second cup of coffee.

"Well, then," she said, "I'll just be—"

He caught her hand before she could escape. And he reeled her in.

Maybe she thought she wasn't going to sleep with

him. But there had been no conditions on kissing or touching or holding her close. He cradled her chin, sliding his fingers under the silky red curls. "What time will you be home?"

"By six or so." She sounded slightly breathless.

He smiled. "I'll go over to the funeral home, take care of things there. And I'll need to make some calls to Chicago. But I'll have most of the day free, until Kim gets home. Anything I can do for you?"

"Do for me?" She was looking at his mouth.

"Pick up your laundry. Run to the store for a carton of milk?"

"Oh, no. But thanks."

"My pleasure."

She lifted her hands, wrapped them around his wrists, as if she meant to pull free of his hold—but then she only held on and stared up at him, her face soft, her lips slightly parted.

He bent his head and kissed those lips. She opened for him, sighing, her hands sliding up to wrap around his shoulders. He gathered her close and tasted her thoroughly.

It didn't matter what she said. They wouldn't last the whole two weeks in separate beds. He gave it two or three days, max. And once they made love again, he felt certain she'd start to see things his way. They'd talk it out and he would convince her that they might as well just go ahead and get married. It would be better for Kim. Better for all of them.

And especially better for the baby.

Because there *was* going to be a baby. Marsh had never felt more certain of anything in his life than of the reality of the child that was coming. He had known it almost from the moment the damn condom broke.

And he accepted it.

He would be a husband to Tory and a father to Kim and the baby. He would have a family—and so would they. He would make right what had gone so wrong ten years ago.

He broke the kiss sooner than he wanted to, showing admirable restraint, he thought. She sighed some more, bending her head so the top of it touched his chin, bringing her hands between them and resting them flat against his chest.

"I have to go," she whispered at the top button of his shirt.

"I know."

But she didn't push at his chest, or give any signal that she wanted him to release her. She looked up at him. "We have to figure out what to tell Kim, about your father."

He nodded at her, pleased that she seemed to find it as difficult to pull away from him as it was for him to keep from touching her. It was kind of a miracle, really, that the thrill of touching her was still there and, if anything, more powerful than it had ever been, after ten full years apart.

She went on, "I was thinking maybe we could have a little talk with her about it tonight. Something simple and to the point. We could say that your father, *her* grandfather, has just died. That he didn't want a funeral, but we are taking his ashes out to the lake this weekend."

The bit about the three of them taking the ashes to the lake was news to him. "We are?"

"I think it would be...a good way to handle it. We could take the ashes out there and say a little prayer and scatter them over the water—that is, if they'll be ready by this weekend."

"I imagine they will. But I'll find out for sure today."

"Then, could we do that, do you think?"

A few golden-red strands of hair had caught on her lashes. He freed them, guided them behind her ear. "Why not?"

"That means yes?"

"Yes. It means yes."

"Your father's house is on the way out there. We could stop in, see if there's anything that should be taken care of there—or maybe you were planning to do that before this weekend?"

"No." He didn't really want to talk about that house. And he certainly had no intention of stopping in there.

"You do have a key?"

He thought of the bag in the trunk of his rental car. His father's pants would be in the bag, and Blake had told him the key was in them. "Yeah."

"Then we could—"

He put a finger to her lips. "I'm not going there, Tory. I'm never going there again. I'll call the utility companies today, see if I can get everything turned off. And then, well, I don't give a damn what happens to that place after that."

"But it belongs to you. It's on five acres, isn't it?"

"How did you remember that?"

"I don't know. You told me once, I guess, all those years ago."

"Well, it's five acres I don't need."

"Marsh. That land is yours. And land values have gone up a lot around here. You should see some of the places they're building out east now. That land is—"

"I said, I don't need it."

"That's not the point. You have to go out there, to go through things, make arrangements to sell it, if that's what you want to do. There will be legal papers. Deeds and such. Did he leave a will?"

"I haven't the faintest idea."

"He would have left everything to you, wouldn't he?"

"That's more or less what he said, yesterday and the day before, when I visited him at the hospital."

"It would be good, though, to see if you could find a will."

"A will doesn't matter. I don't want anything he had to give me. When I left this town ten years ago, I promised myself that no matter what happened—no matter that I was losing you and I didn't know where the hell I was going, no matter that I had nothing but the clothes on my back and the 150 dollars you gave me—no matter how bad it was, there was one good thing, one thing I could be grateful for—that I would never in my life have to see my father's face again, or enter that house I hated so much."

"But, Marsh," she reminded him softly. "You *did*

see your father's face again. You came back when he asked you to."

"Yeah. I did. However rotten he was to me, he was still my father. I felt I owed it to him, to be here for his last days. But the other, the house, it's not an issue."

She touched the side of his face, her hand soft and cool, her expression tender. "Well, Marsh. It seems to me it *is* an issue for you. A big one. If you're afraid to go there—"

He caught her hand. "That's not it. You're not getting it. I'm not *afraid* to go there, I don't *have* to go there. So I'm not *going* to go there."

She pulled her hand free of his grip. "But you can't just—"

"You're wrong. I can. And I will."

"That's childish." She pinched up her mouth at him.

"Call it what you want."

"You not only *own* that property now, Marsh Bravo. You are responsible for it. It doesn't matter what you choose to do with it. You could give it away, if you wanted, to someone who needs it. But it is wrong to just walk away from it, to make the county spend money and effort trying to track you down, then have to condemn it and go through all the processes and paperwork that are required when—"

"Stop." He put his finger against her mouth again. "You know, you really can wear a man down when you set your mind to it."

She looked at him sweetly, from under her lashes. "I am only saying what is right. There was a house on the corner a block away from here that backed up on the creek. It ended up being pretty much abandoned after the woman who owned it died. Her heirs were all the way out in Washington State, I think it was. And they just…ignored the place. The yard grew wild, choked with weeds. Twice a year the city would have to send out a crew to chop everything back. Termites got to it, and at one point there were skunks living in there. Vagrants broke in and set up housekeeping. Finally someone did manage to get hold of the heirs and make an offer they accepted. But that house was a trial to everyone in the neighborhood until then."

She paused, looked at him expectantly—waiting, he knew, for him to give in and see things her way.

When he said nothing, she went into coaxing mode. "Come on. All you really need to do now is check on the place, make sure it's secure, that nothing's leaking or likely to fall in and be a danger."

"A danger to *what?* Tory, that shack of my father's is not in midtown Norman. It's off by itself, out in the woods."

"That's no excuse for completely ignoring it. Just check on it, that's all I'm asking. Then you can let it be, for a while, until you're ready to deal with it."

The irony of the situation didn't escape him. Two things he'd sworn to himself: he would never have to see his father again, and he would never have to go near the tumbledown shack where he'd grown up. But he'd been eighteen then, eighteen and a virtual stranger to the quirks of adult responsibility.

Tory had it right. He might want nothing from

Blake Bravo. But he *was* accountable—accountable as a son. And accountable for his father's house.

"Please, Marsh?"

How could he say no when she asked like that? "All right. In the next few days I'll get out there and have a look around."

Chapter Eleven

Saturday, at ten in the morning, Kim's soccer team, the Red Hornets, played the Moore Lightning Bolts.

Before the game, Marsh met Kim's three best friends. The girls chorused, "Nice to meet you, Mr. Bravo," and then ran off across the soccer field with Kim, to join in on the practice drills.

Tory also introduced him to two of the girls' mothers and one of the dads. They all seemed friendly enough, all older than he and Tory, into their thirties, at least. Clearly, neither Alicia nor Sophie nor Ivy had been born when their parents were still in their teens.

Marsh had vaguely anticipated running into someone he knew at the game, as he had run into Bob Avery at that restaurant on Tuesday. But it didn't happen. Norman was a small town in a lot of ways, but it wasn't *that* small and it was growing all the time.

A man could attend a lot of events without ever running into anyone he knew way back when.

Marsh sat in a folding chair next to Tory and watched his daughter guarding her goal and couldn't help remembering how he used to drive by this sprawling complex of soccer fields and baseball diamonds. That had been in his last couple of years in town, when he'd finally scraped enough together mowing lawns to buy himself some wheels.

Whenever he drove by this place, he would wonder what it would be like to be one of the kids who played soccer or Little League here. To be the kind of kid whose parents signed him up for things and then ferried him around to get to them. The kind of kid whose parents sat on the sidelines at soccer games and cheered when their daughter dived on the ball and kept the other team from scoring—the kind of kid that his own daughter, amazingly, had turned out to be.

The kind of kid the baby would be—he would see to that. He'd had nothing at all to do with Kim turning out happy and well rounded and certain of her place in the world. All the credit there had to go to Tory, and a lot of credit was due. With Kim, now, he hoped he could add something, that he could give her the love and attention only a father can provide—and the opportunities, too.

Not that Tory couldn't provide the opportunities herself. She could. She was a hell of a mother, and it was all too clear that she had enough money. She ran her own business and she'd inherited a fine house in a good neighborhood. She could take care of Kim. He would be here to help now, but the basic job had been done—was being done, and well, without him. Even if he had not returned, Kim would never have lacked for anything.

When it came to the baby, though, he *would* make a difference. For the baby, he could do it all, everything a good father should do. For the baby, he would be there right from the first.

Tory leaped out of the chair beside him. ''Go, Alicia!'' she shouted. ''Kick it! Get that foot on the ball!'' She clapped her hands wildly and let out a whoop.

Kim's little friend gave it a boot, and the ball hit the net. Tory cheered all the louder, only dropping to her chair again after both teams had moved to the center of the field to put the ball back into play.

''Whew.'' She laughed, raising her arms to lift that fiery hair off her neck. The morning sun gleamed off the lenses of her sunglasses. ''I do get excited.''

''Yeah,'' he said low. ''You do.''

Her smile changed, turned soft. Even though he couldn't see her eyes, he knew what was in them. He reached across, snared her hand. She stiffened, marginally, enough so that he could feel the sudden tension in her. But then she relaxed and twined her fingers with his.

For three nights now, he'd slept in the guest room. So far she was holding to her resolve to keep him out of her bed. Every chance he got, he chipped away at that resolve. He stole kisses without shame, pulled her close and wrapped his arms around her whenever he could get her alone.

Last night, after Kim went to bed, they'd necked on

the couch in the family room, like the crazy kids they used to be. It had gotten pretty hot and heavy. At one point, when he had her shirt unbuttoned and her bra undone, when her hand didn't seem to be able to stop itself from flirting with the front of his pants, he'd thought he had it made.

He'd been sure that the time had come, that by tomorrow, which was now today, he'd have gotten a yes out of her—both to lovemaking and to his proposal of marriage.

But then she'd removed her hand from his fly and taken *his* hand out from inside her shirt.

"I'm sorry, Marsh." She was panting, her lips swollen, her cheeks sweetly flushed. "I've let this go way, way too far..." She started squirming around, trying to get her bra hooked again.

He'd wanted to grab her and haul her close again. But he'd held on to his cool, even managed a rueful smile. "I'd say you haven't let it go far enough—and let me help you with that."

She allowed him to hook her bra back up and then she buttoned her shirt again, all the while reminding him of what he didn't need reminding of: the damn agreement to sleep separately.

Once she had her clothes all buttoned and tucked in, she'd offered him coffee. She did that a lot, he'd noticed, offered beverages whenever tensions were high.

Right then, it was fine with him. A beverage sounded pretty damn good. "No coffee, but I wouldn't mind a stiff shot of Jim Beam."

Now, sitting in their matching fold-up lawn chairs

with their fingers intertwined, he could feel her eyes on him. He turned and looked at his reflection in her sunglasses. A tempting smile played on that mouth of hers, and he wanted nothing so much as to lean over and kiss her, deeply. And hard.

But he didn't. Not at their daughter's soccer game. The time for passionate kisses would come again, soon enough.

Tory let him hold her hand until the next time she jumped from her chair to cheer the team on.

The Red Hornets won, six to three. Someone passed out Orange Crush and Twinkie cakes. The parents stood around as the kids devoured their sugary snacks and the coach praised the players. He congratulated Kim on her two best saves, reminded them all to mark their men at throw-ins and not to bunch up on the field.

All the way back to the house, Kim babbled away in the back seat, bragging about her teammates, reliving all the toughest plays. Tory was driving. The light just past the railroad tracks turned red as they reached it. Tory stopped the car.

Kim kept chattering. "Alicia is *so* good. Coach says she has a big foot. And me, too, did you see? When I have to kick it, I can send it all the way down the field."

Tory glanced over at him. She still wore her sunglasses, but it was the same as at the game. Her smile was intimate, just for him.

Things were going well, he decided. Very well.

Soon, she would take him to her bed again. They'd come to another agreement—the *right* one this time.

Kimmy would get her maid-of-honor dress.

And the baby would have what all babies deserve: a mother *and* a father to love and cherish him.

They went to the lake in the afternoon.

The funeral home had given Marsh the ashes on Thursday. Friday he had called the marina and rented them a pontoon boat.

The boat was at Kimmy's request. Wednesday night, when they'd talked about Blake, she had been appropriately solemn at the whole idea of the grandfather she'd never known. Solemn, but not particularly upset. Marsh and Tory had talked about her reaction later, after Kim went to bed. They both admitted they'd feared she might feel cheated somehow, as if they had kept something from her—which they definitely had.

But those were grown-up reactions, they realized after the fact. Kim had never known Blake. And in this she showed a child's wisdom: she didn't presume to miss what she'd never known.

She did, however, become very concerned on the issue of scattering the ashes. She wanted it done right.

And right, to her nine-year-old mind, meant it should be done from a boat. "That way we can be sure that all the ashes get into the lake, because we can go out into the middle, and they will all get in the water before they can get to any dry land. I really think my Bravo grandpa would have wanted that, wanted all the ashes in the water. So, Daddy, will you please find us a boat?"

He couldn't refuse her, though he doubted the old man would have given a damn either way.

The marina lay in a small wooded cove in the Clear Creek arm of the lake. It consisted of a series of covered and open docks connected by plank walkways, boats of different sizes nosed into the docking slots. There was even a parking lot—a bare, hot stretch of flat concrete. Marsh parked the car and they went into the small store/rental office to see about the boat.

Twenty minutes later Marsh was at the rudimentary controls of the pontoon patio boat, which amounted to a large raft with bench seating along the side rails, a picnic table with a bench on either side in the center, a canopy overhead and a series of metal cylinders attached under the water to keep the whole thing afloat.

Piloting the boat was simple. You turned it on and you turned the wheel in whatever direction you wanted it to go. Speed was not an option. The thing crawled the surface of the water like a turtle lumbering along on dry land. They proceeded out of the cove and onto the windblown muddy waters of Lake Thunderbird at a stately pace, which suited the mood of the occasion, not to mention the limited capabilities of the boat.

Kim sat at the side rail, face to the warm wind, wearing denim shorts embroidered with hearts along the hem, a pink shirt and dark glasses with little purple flowers decorating the frames. In her arms she held the terra-cotta urn with her grandfather's ashes in it. Tory sat across from her, all in white, the wind blowing her hair back like a banner of red silk, a white leather Bible clutched in her hand—a Bible, she had told him earlier, that she had received at the age of thirteen on the occasion of joining the Methodist Church.

The boat putted along, cutting the choppy waters in a dogged, relentless fashion. Tory pointed out the family of mud hens wading near the bank and a twisted driftwood log poking out of the water, a gull perched on its topmost point.

Slowly the shore became a shape in the distance. Kim cried out when a large snowy-headed bird plummeted out of the sky a hundred feet from the bow. It slammed the water—and then rose up, a nice-size bass, scales gleaming like splashes of silver in the bright afternoon sun, twisting vainly in powerful talons.

''Bald eagle,'' Tory said. They watched the huge wings beating as the magnificent bird bore its prey away.

''Right there, Daddy!'' Kim cried as the eagle rose high in the sky. ''Right there where the eagle splashed into the water. That's where we should stop. That's where we should let the ashes go.''

Marsh thought wryly that what Kim wanted was more of a tribute than Blake Bravo deserved. Certainly the old man had been a predator. But what kind? A jackal, maybe. Or a hyena. But a majestic eagle? Far from it.

However, Kim didn't know that. And there was no reason she needed to know. If it pleased her to scatter her grandfather's ashes where an eagle had touched down, so be it.

Marsh let off the throttle. They slowed below their former steady crawl. The boat boasted a small anchor. Marsh tossed it over the side when he thought they'd reached the right spot.

Tory opened her Bible. She and Kim had the verses all picked out. Tory read from 2 Samuel, about how we all die and are like water spilled on the ground, impossible to gather up again.

And she read Psalm 23, and the Lord's Prayer and also something that she said was from the book of Job: "I shall go the way whence I shall not return...."

And then she read about how everything has its season.

Finally, she nodded at Kim. "Turn your back to the wind, so it will carry the ashes out over the water."

Kim went to the starboard rail. There, the wind came at her from behind, blowing her hair against her cheeks. Marsh and Tory stood to either side of her. She pulled the big stopper from the wide mouth of the urn.

"Here," said Tory, holding out her hand. Kim gave her the stopper. "Now, tip it flat and shake it."

Kim followed her mother's instructions. What was left of Blake Bravo's body emerged from the mouth of the urn in a gray, grainy cloud. The cloud blew out, making a shadowy film where it landed. In less than a minute it was all gone—all but the thin oily-looking film of ash floating on the wind-rough surface of the water.

They stayed for a little while, out there on the lake, long enough to spot a heron and then an egret gliding along some distance away. Tory had brought a small cooler. They each had a Pepsi. But the mood they shared remained subdued, even reverent.

Marsh felt peaceful within himself when he turned the boat around and started back for the marina.

The peacefulness surprised him. It was not a state he ever would have imagined attaining during any activity even remotely concerning the old man. He supposed he had his daughter and Tory to thank for this, for one memory centering on his father that he could actually treasure. It was a gift, really, and he felt damn grateful.

At least, he felt grateful until they got in the car to go back to the house and Tory asked him if he'd stopped by his father's place to check on things yet.

Chapter Twelve

Tory said, "Did you get by your dad's house yet, to see how things are over there?"

He felt instantly defensive, but he kept his eyes on the road and schooled his voice to sound offhand. "No. Not yet."

He hoped she'd leave it at that. The truth was, he'd already expended more effort than he'd ever planned to on the property he didn't want a damn thing to do with.

It had taken half a day to get things worked out with the utilities.

First of all they'd required proof that Blake had actually died and that Marsh was a close relative—someone likely to have the authority to make the decision to have everything turned off.

So Marsh had had to go and get them what they

needed—his father's death certificate and a copy of his own birth certificate. He'd carried both down to the phone company and to City Hall and to OG&E and OK Natural Gas. It had taken hours of trotting from one agency to another to work it all out. He thought he'd done enough for the time being. He'd get around to visiting the house some other time.

"We could just stop in there now, for a few minutes?" Tory said, her voice rising at the end, making a question when they both knew damn well it wasn't a question at all.

Kim chose that moment to pop open her seat belt and lean between the two front seats. "Yes. I think we should do that. I want to see my Bravo grandpa's house."

Marsh bit back the swear words that rose to his lips. Now he had both of them after him. He sent Tory a quick scowl, one meant to show her just what he thought of her bringing this subject up in front of the kid.

Kim's head was bobbing up and down, as if by nodding furiously, she could further convince them of the wisdom of seeing things her way. "Uh-huh. That's what we should do. I want to see where my Bravo grandpa used to live."

Tory said flatly, "Back in your seat belt, young lady. Now."

Kim let out a little groan but did as she was told. However, as soon as she'd hooked herself in, she started up again. "We said the prayers and we put the ashes out on the lake and that was a good thing. And now I think we should—"

"Kim," Tory said. "That's enough."

Kim let out one small, outraged grunt. Then Marsh heard her flop back hard against the seat, in utter disgust that her wishes were not being taken seriously. But she didn't say anything more.

Too bad there was no one to shut Tory up. "Honestly, Marsh. It would be so easy just to drop by there on the way home..."

He knew he was done for. If he didn't stop at his father's place, he'd have both of them after him now.

Then he made the mistake of glancing Tory's way again. She took off her sunglasses, so he could see the appeal in her gorgeous blue eyes.

He muttered, "All right."

She smiled. Damn. She could turn a man inside out with that smile—but then her brows drew together. "Wait. We'll need a key."

He was sorely tempted to agree with her, to say they'd have to drop by that house some other time. But it would have been a flat-out lie. The bag with the key in it was still in the trunk.

And maybe she was right. They probably *should* have a quick look around the place. Once they did that, he could forget about it for a while.

"I've got one in the trunk," he admitted.

That smile lit up her face again. He turned back to the road before he ran them off it staring at her.

The long dirt driveway that wound off into the trees was so overgrown, Marsh missed it on the first approach. He had to turn the car around and go back, driving at a snail's pace.

Tory spotted it then. She pointed. "Right there."

His heart thudding with a bleak kind of dread he despised himself for feeling, Marsh swung in under the green canopy of blackjack and post oaks. Dogwood branches brushed the sides of the car as they bumped in and out of ruts, and some of the trees hung so low, they scraped the roof.

Marsh tried to keep his mind where it belonged: on him and Tory and Kim, in his rented car, on a sunny Saturday afternoon, driving to his father's house, to make certain that all was in order there.

But the past kept intruding.

More than once he'd fled down this drive as a child, and as a teenager, fled down it in terror, with the old man at his heels, waving a bat or a big stick or even his shotgun, yelling and cursing Marsh for some slight misbehavior—because he had been inattentive when Blake started in on him. Because he'd left his shoes near Blake's favorite chair. Because he frowned when he should have smiled, said nothing when he was expected to answer—or answered when he should have kept his mouth shut.

It had all been the same to Blake. He could go for long stretches of time without resorting to physical violence. He would use his cruel tongue to inflict the damages his mean spirit seemed to demand. But when he decided it was time to get himself a piece of someone's hide, he went after it with gusto.

Blake had chased Marsh's mother down this drive, too. Marsh had a swift, stunning vision: his mother, in her nightgown, racing away under the oaks, her bare legs flashing blue-white in the darkness.

He blinked. He didn't even remember what that had been about—the night his mother ran screaming from the house—didn't recall what had set his father off that time, to make him go after her, to make her so scared that she ran out in her nightclothes. But then, what did it matter what small transgression she'd committed?

It didn't. It never had.

He turned the last curve in the drive and there was the house, such as it was, crouched under the oaks ahead, looking about the same as he remembered it, weathered clapboard, once painted white, but with most of the paint peeled off years ago. A jut of porch roof on two rough posts, hanging out over the front door.

It had changed very little since the last time he'd seen it, the night he had turned on the old man....

It was about money, that time—the money Marsh had earned himself, mowing lawns and trimming hedges for people who lived a much better life than he'd ever known. Blake wanted to know where Marsh kept that money. Marsh swore there was no money. And there wasn't. He'd spent what he'd saved on his car and then on gas and repairs. It could get expensive, keeping an old car running. And then, whatever money was left, he spent on Tory, so they could go to a movie now and then, or out for a hamburger and a shake.

Blake said, "It's that damn car, isn't it?" He said he was going to take Marsh's car and sell it, that Marsh owed him that, for feeding him and putting clothes on his sorry back for the past eighteen years.

Marsh dared to say no—that the car was his, he'd

paid for it himself, and his father would never get his greedy hands on it. Blake went ballistic. And Marsh fought back. It was all a blur now, the part where he'd started hitting and never wanted to stop.

When he did stop, he was standing over the old man. The old man was out cold. And there was blood.

He called an ambulance, babbled something into the phone about a bad fall, an injured man and the address of his father's house. Then he ran outside, jumped in his car and took off backward down the driveway, out to the road.

But he couldn't quite make himself leave without knowing that some kind of help had come.

He drove the car off the road, into the shelter of the trees, where no one would be likely to notice it at first glance. Then he ran back up the driveway and around the back of the house, into the dark haven of the woods.

He would never forget the high, wild screams of the sirens as they came on, the way the red-and-blue flashing lights had made the tree shadows jiggle and shimmy in an eerie, otherworldly looking dance. He'd hidden crouched in the undergrowth until they'd put Blake's still form in the ambulance and driven away, until the two policemen, who had shown up right after the paramedics, had had a good look around and decided there was nothing else they could do that night. One of the cops had checked things out behind the house, bouncing a flashlight beam from tree to tree. Marsh had huddled down among the sumac and dewberry bushes, close to the mulch smell of damp earth and rotting leaves, staying clear of that beam.

Finally, when the wailing of the sirens had faded off into the night and the cops had driven their patrol car away down the twisting drive, when the renewed hooting of the owls and the trilling of a whippoorwill had told him it was safe, Marsh had emerged from the trees. He'd fled down the drive for the last time, thinking of Tory. Of saying goodbye…

Marsh stopped the car in front of the shed several yards from the main house. His father's ancient pickup, painted primer gray and rusting in places in spite of the primer coat, waited under the carport that jutted off the side of the shed.

It would wait forever now. Blake Bravo would never again slide in behind the wheel and roar off down the drive.

From the back seat Kim said in a slightly awe-struck tone, "Everything looks kind of *old*."

Old was one way of putting it.

Rundown, derelict and *ramshackle* were a few more.

Rejected tools and equipment sat out at the mercy of the elements, from several rotted tires of varying sizes leaning up against the side of the shed to the wringer washing machine half-buried a few feet from the tires. Beside the washer, there was an old tin tub, half-filled with brackish water. Over by the house Marsh spotted a Weed Eater and a straight chair with one leg missing, listing sadly to the side. There was also a rake minus most of its prongs.

And there were stacks of empty plastic pots, the black ones you get at nurseries when you buy a plant—lots of plastic pots, but not a plant in sight that didn't look as if it had grown there wild, at nature's urging, with no help from human hands. To keep the fire danger down during the dry months, his father might use the Weed Eater now and then, but he'd never been one inclined to cultivating. Things either grew or they didn't, and Blake Bravo didn't much care either way.

Tory set her dark glasses in the little slot beneath the stereo control panel. "I'd forgotten..." she said softly, her voice fading off at the end. She was lucky. Marsh would never forget.

He reached down beside his left foot and popped the trunk latch. Then they all three got out of the car, emerging into the sounds of crows cawing, blue jays squawking at each other and the rat-tat-tat of a woodpecker going to work on a tree trunk not too far away. A fox squirrel zipped across the cleared space between the house and the shed, pausing once at the midway point to dart a glance left and right and give a couple of flicks to its bushy red tail.

"What about animals?" Kim asked, looking up at Marsh. "Aren't there some animals? Out here, you could even have a horse."

Marsh hid a smile. His father would have been no more likely to keep a horse or a cow than to plant a fruit tree and water it when it was dry. Blake Bravo didn't cultivate. And animal husbandry was a subject for off-color jokes to him, and no more.

"No, I don't think so," Marsh said. "There's just the house and the shed and five acres of woods, the way I remember it."

"Maybe a dog?" Kim suggested hopefully.

Marsh shook his head.

Kim kept on hoping. "A cat, then?"

Marsh remembered his mother's big white cat, Fluffy. Blake had had no use for Fluffy—and Fluffy had disappeared when Marsh was eight.

"No," Marsh told his daughter. "I don't think we're going to find any cats here—unless some stray has taken up residence since your grandpa went to the hospital."

Kim's dark eyes widened. "Maybe we'll find a stray kitten. If we did, we'd have to take it home and adopt it, we couldn't just leave it here for some wild animal to gobble up."

"We're not taking any kittens home," Tory warned.

"But Mom—"

"We're here to check on your Bravo grandpa's house. Period." Kim scrunched up her nose, but didn't say any more. Tory turned to Marsh. "The key?" She said it softly, as if she knew just exactly how he felt about going under the rickety porch overhang and into the house where he'd finally ended up beating his father senseless.

"Right." He went around to the trunk, lifted the lid and grabbed the bag by the bottom, dumping the contents out on the trunk floor.

He looked down at the things that had spilled from the bag. There was a faded pair of jeans, lace-up work boots, a chambray shirt, underwear, a battered leather wallet and a dime-store watch. Marsh picked up the jeans and felt in the pockets until he came up with a plain metal key ring that held four keys—two of them, he knew, would open the house and the shed. The third went to the pickup. He had a pretty good idea what the fourth key would open.

And he would find out for certain soon enough.

He stuck the keys in his pocket, shoved everything else back into the bag and shut the lid to the trunk.

After that there was nothing else to do but go into the house.

The front door opened right onto the living area, which was as he remembered it: brown. A dark-brown carpet speckled with lint, his father's brown corduroy recliner, a grungy looking tan sofa, a coffee table of dark-stained oak. And a television on a metal stand, the same television that had been there ten years before. The walls had once been off-white, but it was so long since they'd seen fresh paint they had achieved the same dingy tan as the sofa. There was a large watermark on the ceiling.

"Roof leak," Tory said, looking up.

Marsh said nothing. He expected her to start in on how he'd have to do something about that, and when she did, he was planning to ignore her, no matter how hard she pushed.

But she didn't say more and he told himself to be thankful for that.

The place smelled damp and sour. Kim sniffed the air and made a face. But her good upbringing showed: she didn't announce, as some children might have, "It stinks in here."

Tory flicked the wall switch and the light came on. She sent him a questioning look, which he read without her having to say a word.

"They told me they probably wouldn't get around to turning the lights off for another week or two."

Tory frowned. "That reminds me. The refrigerator. We can't just leave it to rot when the power goes off. We'll have to clean it out."

No, we won't, he thought. We won't *have* to do a damn thing.

"And what about a freezer?" Tory asked. "Did your dad have one?"

He looked at her, dead-on, and muttered, "Yeah."

"Then we'll have to take care of that, too."

No way. "I'll take care of it, next week."

She didn't believe he had any intention of taking care of it next week, he could see it in those eyes of hers. "Marsh, really. If we look around now, we can probably find a few empty boxes. We could—"

"I said I'd take care of it. And I will. I'll call a temp agency and have someone sent out here to do everything that needs doing."

She looked at him for a long moment, then seemed to realize that there were some points beyond which he would not be pushed. She shrugged and moved on, toward the open arch that framed the kitchen. He decided he wouldn't even go in there. It had been in there that the last battle with Blake had occurred. Kim's small hand slid into his. "Come on, Daddy. The kitchen..."

He looked down at his daughter and made his mouth form a smile. "Your mama can handle things in there. I'm going to check down the hall."

Kim wrapped her hand around his index finger. "I'll go with you."

A natural urge to protect rose in him. He started to tell her to stay where she was.

But then he realized his own foolishness. The only danger here lay in the ugliness of certain memories, memories of which his daughter was entirely unaware—thank God.

"Okay," he said. "Let's go."

There were three bedrooms, with one small bath at the end of the hall. Marsh flicked on the light in his father's room and looked inside. Nothing new there: a double bed, two pasteboard bureaus and a window air conditioner. They went on, to the second bedroom, which had once been Marsh's. His bed was still there, and so was his dresser, along with stacks of boxes lined up along one wall. Apparently, Blake had been using that room for storage.

He turned off the light, and he and Kim moved on to the bathroom, where the shower curtain had mold on it and the sink faucet steadily leaked onto a big rust spot in the bowl of the sink. The leak was no problem, he though with some irony. It would be fixed in a few days when the water went off.

The final bedroom, across the hall from Marsh's old room, was locked with a padlock. This did not surprise Marsh. The room was Blake's "office," his private sanctuary. Blake had always kept it locked up tight. He'd even had bars installed on the windows, which faced the woods.

Marsh fingered the key ring in his pocket. Old fears were rousing, tightening his stomach and making a sour taste in his mouth. Those fears no longer applied, but somehow that didn't stop them from finding him.

You didn't go into the old man's office, not unless you wanted to get whupped and whupped good.

Yes, Marsh knew very well that Blake Bravo was no longer around to whup anybody. But he'd been trained too well.

And besides, he didn't give a damn what was behind that door. He didn't want anything to do with his father's sick secrets.

"Daddy?" Kim squeezed his finger. "Do you have the key?"

"There were several on that ring," Tory said. He turned to find her standing behind them—apparently finished with checking out the kitchen and ready to poke that pretty freckled nose into something more interesting.

He knew he was trapped. He did not want her to find out how he felt right then—sick to his stomach, plain sick at heart. Didn't want her—or Kimmy, either, for pity's sake—to know how much of a hold his father's various cruelties still had on him.

He took the key ring from his pocket.

It was an easy match. The smallish brass-colored key would be the one.

And it was. He opened the padlock and undid the hasp. Then he pushed open the door.

The room beyond was dim, the curtains drawn.

There was a twin set of two-decker file cabinets, a Smith-Corona electric typewriter on a rickety stand and a metal bookcase, the shelves stacked with newspapers and magazines. These things Marsh had expected.

What he hadn't expected was the state-of-the-art computer, complete with giant-size monitor and multifunction printer that sat on the battered metal desk. The computer had been left on, the monitor displaying a screen saver of fish in an aquarium. The speakers, turned down low, emitted bubbling, glugging underwater sounds.

Marsh could see the phone hookup emerging from the back of the impressive machine. Leave it to Blake. Rabbit ears on his prehistoric television, but he was hooked into the Internet. If he'd only been a little closer in to town, he'd probably be on a DSL line.

Marsh noted the new air conditioner, humming away in the window, keeping the air reasonably free of humidity and the pricey equipment nice and cool.

Kim said, "Wow. That's a *big* computer."

Marsh made himself step into the room. He turned off the air conditioner. All the computer cables fed into a backup box, a big one that would keep the thing running for some specified amount of time if the power went off. He switched off the backup box. The screen went black and the glugging whisper from the speakers was no more.

Tory said, "Marsh. Are you sure you should—"

He silenced her with a look. Then he knelt and pulled the backup box plug from the wall. That accomplished, he rose to his height. "We are finished here."

They fell back from the doorway as he came toward them, both of them watching him through wide, solemn eyes. He put the lock back in place and snapped it shut. "Let's go."

Neither of them said a word as he herded them ahead of him, down the short, dim hall, out through the bleak brown living room to the front door.

Chapter Thirteen

That night, after Kim was in bed, Tory brought up the question of Blake's mail.

"We should have checked your father's mailbox," she said.

They were sitting on the sofa in the family room, the sofa where he'd almost managed to get her bra off the night before. He had his arm around her and her head was on his shoulder and he was feeling pretty good—or he had been until the subject of Blake Bravo had reared its ugly head again.

Tory pulled away, putting her hand against his chest and craning back enough that she could look at him. "You know, I don't even remember seeing a mailbox."

He let out a weary breath. "Because there wasn't one. My father didn't have his mail delivered. He kept a P.O. box—though he never would say where, specifically.''

''At the downtown post office, do you think?''

''Could be.''

Her eyes were very bright. ''I know. You could go talk to one of the utility companies again. You could ask them for the P.O. box where your father had them send the bill. Then you'd know which post office to talk to about rerouting his mail so that you can take care of it.''

He made sure she was through talking before he said, very clearly, ''No.''

She caught her lower lip between her teeth and her lashes swept down, then up, a hesitant, thoroughly charming action that communicated how very reluctant she was to pressure him on this subject.

Not quite hesitant enough, however, because she said, ''Marsh, I really think this is something you should check into.''

He decided it was time to get a few things clear between them. He captured both her hands in his. ''Tory, listen.''

She looked at him sideways, suspiciously. ''What?''

''Are you listening?''

''Of course.'' She gave a little tug on her hands, but he ignored it and held on.

He said, gently, ''I've taken all the responsibility I intend to right now, when it comes to my father's worldly goods. I've arranged it so things will be turned off at the house, and we've checked to see that everything's in reasonable order there. Next week, I'll get the food cleaned out of the freezer and the refrigerator. That's more than enough for now."

"But I just think..." She let the thought trail off.

He knew he shouldn't ask, but he did it anyway. "You think what?"

She scanned his face. "Aren't you...curious? About him? I mean, who really knew him? What was he like, deep down, in his most secret self?"

"Tory, what Blake Bravo was like deep down is something I honestly do not want to know."

"I can see that. And I just don't understand it. If I were you, I'd be going crazy to find out everything I could."

"Well, guess what? You're not me."

"Oh, I know. But...that locked room. I keep thinking about it. All those stacks of newspapers and magazines, the file cabinets, that incredible computer... Oh, Marsh, you could probably learn a lot about him, if you would only—"

He was shaking his head. "Tory."

"I just think that you—"

"No."

Those red lashes swept down again. And when her eyes met his he saw that she had finally heard him, finally accepted that she couldn't make him do a thing just because it was what she would want to do.

"Okay." She said the word on a breath. "I'll leave it alone."

"Thank you."

Her sweet, soft mouth was only inches from his. He bent forward and pressed his lips to hers. She sighed and gave another tug on her hands. He let them go and wrapped his arms around her, smiling against her mouth as her hands pressed first against his chest, then slid up to clasp around his neck.

The kiss lasted a long time—but it was still way too short in his opinion. Too soon she was pulling back, offering beverages.

He knew what it meant when she brought up the beverages. Another night that was not going to end up being *the* night.

He said yes to club soda with lime.

Monday, Marsh flew back to Chicago. He had a few fires to put out at Boulevard. He arrived back in Oklahoma City on Wednesday at eleven in the morning, picked up a fresh car at the airport and drove straight to Norman.

It was a little before noon when he pulled up in front of Tory's house. He'd left the garage remote behind, so he had to go in the front door. As he strode up the walk, suitcase in hand, Rayanne Pickett came out of the house next door.

She trotted right over to him across her smooth green lawn. "Marsh Bravo. Wait a minute, please."

He stopped, waited for her to get to him, then asked politely, "How are you, Mrs. Pickett?"

"I'm doin' okay," she said briskly, tipping her head back to look at him, shading her eyes with a perfectly manicured, ring-laden hand. She was a short, sturdy woman, with a deep tan and chin-length hair that was still the same shade of golden blond he remembered. No doubt she kept it that way with regular visits to a favorite beautician, since she had to be at least into her sixties by now.

"I wonder," she said, "if you would mind coming over to my house for a few minutes. I would like to speak with you."

He didn't like the tightly wound sound of her voice. And he suspected he wasn't going to like hearing whatever she had to say, either.

But he went with her, anyway, thinking that he might as well give her a chance to lay it all out on the table—and maybe secretly hoping he had it all wrong, that she was just going to offer him some refreshments and make a little small talk, to play the friendly neighbor and then send him on his way.

She did offer refreshments, but she had more on her mind than making small talk. However, it was not immediately apparent exactly what she'd dragged him into her living room to say.

She kept circling the subject. "Mr. Bravo, I have to tell you, Tory is like a daughter to me. And I think of Kim as I think of my own grandchildren. And I…well, you might remember that I've been widowed for fifteen years now. I don't know how I would have gotten through it, at first, without Audra and Seth Winningham living next door to me, treating me like a part of their family. I feel I owe them…and that includes their daughter and their granddaughter. I, well, I want you to understand."

He sipped lemonade and nodded. "I think I do understand, Mrs. Pickett."

"Tory is doing so well now. But I don't think you can have any idea what it was like for her, ten years ago, after you...'' She seemed to be seeking the right words.

He decided he might as well provide them. ''Ran out on her?''

Diamond rings glittering, Rayanne Pickett waved a hand. ''Now, now. I didn't say that. I understand that your home life was...well, that it was just terrible. Tory did confide a little in her mother. And Audra felt she could talk to me. So I got some of the story, at least. And I am...well, I am sympathetic to what you've been through, I truly am. I can't even imagine how awful it must have been for you. But you *did* disappear, for ten long years. And Tory and Kim had to learn to get along without you.''

He set down his lemonade on a snow-white stone coaster. The living room was all done in white and gold, with two big soft white sofas, and easy chairs that were in white velvet and gold brocade. He had begun to find the room *too* white, and the chair he sat in way too soft.

Rayanne said, ''They've been doing just fine, Tory and Kim, all on their own.''

He longed for her to get to the point. ''Mrs. Pickett, everything you're saying, I already know.''

She coughed again, then folded her hands in her lap. She looked down at all those diamonds clustered on her fingers, as if she drew strength from the sight of them. Then she pulled her shoulders back and sat tall in her soft white chair. ''Well, I just don't know how to say this. I just don't see how I can stand by and do nothing, when I am so worried about what's going to happen now, about what you're up to, staying in the

Winninghams' house. About whether you're going to break poor Tory's heart all over again.''

Marsh studied the woman. Strangely, he didn't feel angry with her. She seemed...kinder, really, than he remembered. A well-meaning person doing what she thought was right. He found he wished he had some answers for her. But he was afraid he'd only make things worse if he explained the situation, if he told her that he and Tory had an agreement: she'd marry him when she found out for sure that he'd made her pregnant.

That would go over like a keg party at church.

Better to skip the explanations and find out what Rayanne Pickett actually intended to do. ''Mrs. Pickett, is this some kind of *warning* you're giving me?''

The plump ringed fingers went to her throat. ''Well, I...I do think I will have to call Audra and Seth. I think they should know what's going on. And I wanted to be fair, to face you and tell you just what I intend to do.''

''Have you told Tory?''

''Well, no. I have not. I just realized, when I saw you coming up the Winninghams' front walk a few minutes ago, what I would do. I am going to do it soon. Today. I am telling you. I'm certain you will tell Tory.''

She was wrong there. He wouldn't tell Tory. It would feel too much like carrying tales. He'd just let the whole thing play itself out. Tory's parents would learn that he'd come back into her life again, anyway, as soon as he and Tory found out for sure about the baby, when they started making plans for the wedding.

And now that he thought about it, shouldn't they know about him already? He'd been staying in Tory's house for a week now. But Tory never mentioned them, never said she'd called them or that they'd called her, never let him know she'd told them that their granddaughter's father was back in town.

But then again, maybe she'd talked to them yesterday or Monday, while he was in Chicago. Maybe she'd talked to them earlier, told them about his visit, and just not mentioned it to him.

And that brought to mind another uncomfortable question: Why would she avoid mentioning that she'd talked to them? Unless her parents had said things she didn't want to repeat to him.

Rayanne was staring down at her rings again. "Tory may be angry with me. I'm sure she will be. But I have to do what I think is right."

Marsh stood. "Thanks for the lemonade, Mrs. Pickett."

Tory drove home from the shop that evening feeling terrific. Marsh should be back by now. She had missed him and she couldn't wait to see him again.

He should be there, at the house, when she arrived. Kim would be off with her friends at soccer practice. They'd have a few minutes alone before one of them went to pick up the girls at the practice field.

When she pulled into the garage and saw his rental car already inside, Tory's heart seemed to get bigger inside her chest. My, my. She was just bursting with happiness at the thought that he was home again.

Home again.

Oh, yes. She was starting to think of her home as Marsh's home, too. And she was finding that she *liked* thinking of it that way.

She found him sitting out in back, on the bench under the mulberry tree, with Mr. Pickles lying in the thick grass a few feet away. He watched her coming toward him across the lawn, and she thought he looked a little...distant. A little drawn into himself.

Maybe it was the way he just sat there, looking at her, making no move to rise, to invite her into his arms.

Usually, every chance he got he would take her in his arms. She'd grown accustomed to displays of affection from him, and now, when one wasn't forthcoming, it took her by surprise, made her feel off balance, and more than a little shy.

She sat on the bench beside him. ''Hi.''

The day was warm, in the mid-eighties, and humid. But there was something cool and dry about the smile he gave her.

''How was your flight?''

''Uneventful.''

''Everything...all right?''

''Sure. Everything's fine. Why?''

''You seem...I don't know. A little distant.''

He looked across the yard, toward the house. ''I was just sitting here thinking how some things never change.''

She didn't know what to say to that, so she said nothing.

He continued in a musing tone, his gaze still focused on the house, ''You painted the front door green and put flower beds in front of the windows, but it's still the same house, isn't it? The same grass I used to mow. And you're the same nice girl you always were. A *good* girl, from a good family.''

Something was definitely bothering him. ''Marsh. What's the matter?''

''I was just wondering...''

''What?''

He turned and looked at her, his eyes probing. ''How are your parents, anyway?''

She frowned. ''My parents? They're...well, they're just fine, as far as I know.''

''When was the last time you talked to them?''

''Well, it was...over a week ago, now that you mention it.''

''How surprising.'' Sarcasm dripped from the words.

''Marsh. What is the matter?''

A thin brown bird with a long tail and a slightly hooked beak lit on the lawn across the yard. It strutted toward the holly tree in the far corner, head bobbing back and forth with each step. Mr. Pickles watched it through slitted green eyes, his long tail twitching lazily.

Marsh still hadn't answered her. She looked at him again. ''Marsh?''

He shrugged. ''It's just strange to me, that's all. Your daughter's father comes back, after all these years, and somehow you don't get around to letting your parents in on the news.''

Well, Tory thought, he has hit the bull's-eye with that one.

She tried not to look as guilty as she felt. She wasn't exactly eager to tell her parents about Marsh. They still thought of him as the confused, deeply damaged boy who had gotten their darling only daughter pregnant and then run off and left her to have a baby on her own.

Eventually, of course, she would straighten them out. As soon as they had a chance to spend a little time with him, they'd realize what a fine man he'd become.

But it was not going to be pleasant at first.

Marsh muttered, "Just like old times, don't you think?"

Her guilt faded a little. Irritation took its place. "What are you trying to say, Marsh?"

"Guess."

"You are playing mean word games, and I don't like it one little bit."

"Well, all right. Let me put it this way. I was your naughty secret then—and look at us now."

She felt the hot blush sweep upward over her cheeks and didn't know whether it was from righteous anger—or from shame. "You are twisting everything. Why are you doing that? You never used to—"

"Right," he said, his voice low and soft and not kind at all. "I never used to throw it up to you, how far I was beneath you. That you wouldn't face down your parents for me, that the only way you would see me was by sneaking around. Back then I was just grateful that someone like you would even *look* at me. Every moment I spent with you was like some special, beautiful gift. That you would even let me touch you, that seemed like a miracle to a loser like me—and I've been sitting here, thinking about that, wondering if maybe you *liked* it, being a nice girl with a back-door boyfriend, if it excited you."

She could hardly believe he was saying these cruel things. "Marsh, that is not true."

"Oh, come on. You were slumming with me, having yourself a little walk on the wild side."

She jerked back as if he had slapped her—and then she made herself peer more closely at him. "What happened today? Something happened, didn't it, to make you angry with me?" He looked away. She said, "I guess you will tell me, when you're good and ready to."

He said nothing. She knew then that she had gotten near the truth. Something had happened to upset him, and for some reason he wasn't willing to tell her what.

She touched his arm, felt the hard muscle go even harder as he stiffened. But he didn't pull away. She decided that was something. "Marsh."

He still didn't speak, and he didn't turn toward her. But he did allow her to keep holding his arm.

"You're right, Marsh. You did excite me back then. We both know you did. But it wasn't for the reasons that you just said. It was...because you were always so tender with me. Because when I looked in your eyes, I saw goodness—and how much you wanted me. I have to admit. That made me feel powerful, that you saw me as beautiful, that you wanted me so much. I did feel that I was the one...in control. Well, I mean, if either of us was. And maybe, in some ways, I took advantage of you."

Slowly he turned his head. He was looking at her now. “*You* took advantage of *me?* Is that what you just said?”

She nodded. “Well, we both know how it was, don’t we, those three times that we messed up? We both know how you kept saying we shouldn’t, and I kept saying we wouldn’t…and then, in the end, I *was* the one who took the lead. You were always willing to stop, any time I had said I didn’t want to go any further. You stopped all those other times, when I told you we had to.”

He was smiling again—a much warmer smile than before. “So you’re saying you seduced me.”

She let go of his arm and wrinkled her nose at him. “I’m saying that I admit we might never have gone all the way if I hadn’t been so…enthusiastic about it. But it wasn’t some cheap thrill for me. I was with you because I loved you and wanted you and felt so darn wonderful whenever you touched me.”

“Well,” he said, and guided a corkscrew of hair behind her ear. “All right.”

She felt a few words of reproach were in order. “You ought to be ashamed of yourself, for thinking such mean things about me.”

He looked wonderfully contrite. “I am ashamed. I apologize.”

She made a little humphing sound.

“Come on, say you forgive me.”

“Oh, all right.” She gave him a look from under her lashes. “I forgive you.”

“Thank you—and you can seduce me again. Anytime. I’m willing.”

"I'm glad."

"Are you?" His eyes looked sad, all of a sudden.

"Oh, Marsh. Yes, I am. And I'd be all over you, you know I would—but we do have a nine-year-old to consider now."

He bent closer. "Not right this minute, we don't."

She took his wrist and looked at his Rolex. "No. But in ten minutes, we do. One of us has to get over to Brookhaven Park and pick her up—and the other girls, too."

"One of us. I know what that means. It's not going to be you."

"I was thinking I could get the dinner on the table..."

"Got it all planned out, haven't you? Sounds to me like you're *still* the one in control."

"Oh, right. Like I control *you.* I don't, and we both know I don't."

"I have noticed that things generally seem to go the way that *you* want them to."

"Oh, really? You think so?"

"See? You can't quite make yourself lie outright and say it isn't true."

She made a small, self-satisfied noise in response to that remark. Marsh bent forward a fraction more.

And then he was kissing her.

They sat there on that bench and kissed for all they were worth for the full ten minutes until Marsh had to go and pick up the girls. She never got around to asking him again what it was that had upset him so.

Her mother called at eight-thirty that night.

Chapter Fourteen

They were just cleaning up the dinner dishes. Tory stood at the sink, loading the dishwasher. Kim and Marsh were clearing the table.

And the phone rang.

Kim sang out, "I'll get it!" She dropped the salad bowl she'd just picked up and raced around the table to grab the receiver off the wall. "Hello, Winningham residence, Kimberly speaking," she announced, showing off the flawless phone etiquette that Tory had taken such pains to drill into her over the years.

Kim's face lit up. "Grandma Audra!"

Tory grabbed a towel and looked at Marsh. His eyes were waiting. She sent him what she hoped was a reassuring smile as she hung the towel back on the rack. Her silly stomach had gone all jittery with what she knew was plain old dread.

Kim started chattering away. ''How *are* you, Grandma?...Oh, I am just fine.... Yes, I have been doing real good at school, even with math, and the Red Hornets won the game on Saturday. You should have seen me. I made some *major* saves.... Uh-huh... Yes, I did. Oh, and Grandma Audra, guess what?''

Tory knew what was coming.

''My daddy came home.'' Kim glanced up, aimed her shining smile at Marsh, who gamely smiled back at her. ''Yes,'' Kim said into the phone. ''Yes, he did.... He is here now and he stays in the guest room. I also had a Bravo grandpa, did you know that? But he died and we took his ashes and put them out on the lake at a place where an eagle landed. Then we went to his *house*. It was *old* and he didn't even have a cat or a dog, but he had a *big* computer and... What?... Oh, okay. Love you. Say I love you to Grandpa Seth. All right. Hold on.''

Kim put her hand over the receiver and announced in a loud whisper, ''It's Grandma Audra.''

''No kidding,'' Tory said, managing to sound calm and unruffled, though her stomach had gone from jittery to outright churning.

''She wants to talk to you.'' Kim held out the phone.

Tory shot another glance Marsh's way. She did not want to have this particular conversation with either Marsh or Kim listening in.

Marsh seemed to know what she was thinking. ''Go ahead,'' he said. ''Take it in the bedroom.''

Her mother's first question was more or less what Tory had expected.

"Honey, are you sure you know what you are doing?"

"Yes, Mama. I do. I know exactly what I'm doing."

"Oh, honey..."

"Don't worry. Please. Everything is going to be fine."

"Is it?"

"Yes."

"Now, honey, I don't think you're looking at this with a logical mind."

Tory gritted her teeth and dropped to the edge of the bed. "What are you getting at, Mama?"

"Well, it's just that, I'm sure it must seem very...romantic to you, to have that boy show up again, after all these years."

"Mama, Marsh is not a *boy*. He's twenty-eight years old and he—"

"All right, honey. He's a *man* now. I'm not disputin' that point at all. And I also know that all the troubles he had as a boy weren't really his fault. But you cannot deny the facts. And the facts are that he did run away, he...injured that awful father of his and then he left town. He left you and he deserted his child."

"That is not fair. He didn't even know about Kim. You know that he didn't."

Silence hummed down the line. Then her mother allowed, "Well, all right. He didn't know about Kimmy. But he did take advantage of you."

"Mama. He did not take advantage of me. I loved him. And he loved me."

"Oh, honey, I just don't think a man like that is someone you should have staying in your home."

Tory's nerves were just humming. She couldn't sit still. She stood. "He happens to be my daughter's father."

"Well, I know that, sweetheart."

Tory paced the small sitting area between the bed and the door. "And he is—and always was—a good person."

Her mother made a sniffing sound. "I understand that that father of his has died."

"Yes. Of a heart attack, a week ago Tuesday. There was no funeral. That was how Blake wanted it."

Her mother made the proper noises of regret. "Well, I am sorry to hear of his death."

Tory said what was expected of her. "I'll give Marsh your condolences."

"Oh, Tory. Your father and I have just been worried sick."

Tory stopped in midstride. "What did you say, Mama?"

"I said, your father and I have been—"

"Since *when* have you been worried sick?"

"Well, since this afternoon, when we talked to Rayanne."

"Rayanne called you to talk to you about Marsh staying with me and Kim?"

"Get that tone out of your voice right now. You don't have to go and get mad at Rayanne. She did what she thought was right and I'm glad she did. You should have done it. *You* should have called us and told us what was going on."

Tory had no comeback for that. She *should* have called them. She'd gained nothing by dodging this issue with them. She'd only made things worse.

Her mother went on. "And Rayanne didn't go behind anyone's back, either. She told that boy—excuse me—that *man*, this afternoon what she was going to do. She said that he was quite...polite about the whole thing, which I have to say has been the only bright spot in all of this. Rayanne said he was polite and he *looked* real good. As if maybe he has done all right for himself."

"He has," Tory said proudly, grabbing the opportunity to praise Marsh to her mother, telling herself to forget for the moment that Marsh had had some run-in with Rayanne and hadn't even mentioned it to her. "He's done more than all right. He owns his own company, Boulevard Limousine of Chicago. And he's been to college, he has a four-year degree."

Audra took a moment to digest that information. Then she said with infuriating carefulness, "I suppose you know that because he *told* you so."

Tory got busy mentally counting to ten. "Yes, Mama. That's right. He told me so. And I happen to *trust* him."

Her mother clucked her tongue.

Tory took in a breath, let it out slowly. "We're... getting to know each other again. You should see him with Kim. He's just crazy about her, and she feels the same about him."

"Well and that's very nice, but you have to be *careful,* Victoria. You have to consider what happened in the past, that you are vulnerable to this person and that you just can't let him take advantage of you, you can't let him move in on you.''

''He is not *moving in* on me, Mama. I was the one who invited him to stay here. And I'm glad I did.''

''How long is he staying?''

She thought of the agreement, of the baby that might even now be growing inside her. ''At least another week or so.''

''He's staying with you for two *weeks?* How does he run that company he told you he owns if he's staying in Norman for all that time?''

''Mama. This conversation is getting us nowhere.''

''I think your father and I should fly back home right away.''

''No.'' Tory made her voice flat and firm.

''But I—''

''Mama, not only is Marsh a man now, *I* am a woman. I make my own decisions and, while I do love and respect you and Daddy and think the world of your good opinion, you just don't run my life anymore. I don't want you to come home right now. This is a time for Marsh and me and Kim. Please. You are just going to have to trust my judgment on this.''

''Honey, you have a child to think about.''

''I *am* thinking of my child.''

''Victoria. Are you...? Lord forgive me, I have to ask. Kimberly said he was staying in the guest room. But are you...sleepin' with him? Are you letting him take advantage of you all over again?''

''Mama.'' Tory dropped to the small easy chair opposite the door. ''Mama, you have gone too far.''

''Honey, I just—''

"I am going to hang up now."

"Wait. Please. Just wait a minute.... I...I am sorry. That question was one I never should have asked."

"You're right. You should not have. And I mean it, Mama. Don't come here. Maybe in a few weeks, we'll...invite you to our wedding." There. It was out. And she found she was *glad* it was out.

"You're talking of *marriage?*"

"Yes. We are."

"Well. I don't know what to say."

"Say you love me. Say you trust me."

"Well, I do love you, dear. And you know that I trust you."

"Good. And you were right about one thing. I should have called you, should have told you what was going on. I regret that I didn't."

"Yes, well. You certainly should have. Tory..."

"What, Mama?"

"Do not hesitate to call us. If you need us. For anything."

"I won't. I love you."

"And we love you, too."

As soon as Kim was in bed, Marsh asked Tory to go out onto the back patio with him. They sat in the padded chairs, at the table with the glass top, as they had that first night he had spent in her house, one week and one day before.

Tory knew why he'd asked her to go outside. He wanted to make certain Kim couldn't hear what they said.

It was a warm night, the air sweet and thick. Crickets chirped in the damp grass. The long, clicking song of a cicada came from somewhere near the back fence. As a rule, Tory found night sounds soothing.

But not right then. She was all nerves by then. Marsh had seemed way too quiet since her mother's phone call. And Tory had had to keep reminding herself not to jump to conclusions. Just because he wasn't yakking his head off didn't necessarily mean he was upset with her.

She'd no sooner settled into her chair than it occurred to her that he might want something to drink.

"Would you like some cold tea, Marsh? Or maybe a Pepsi?" She started to rise.

He put his hand over hers. "No more beverages. Sit back down."

She dropped to the chair again and frowned at him. No more beverages. That was an odd way of putting it.

He squeezed her hand, then let go of it. "You always want to bring on the beverages whenever you're nervous."

"I do?"

"You do." He sat back in his chair.

Tory sat back, too, trying to relax a little, trying not to be quite as nervous as they both knew she was. As before, she had left the lights on inside. It was enough light to see by, and the darkness was peaceful—and peacefulness was something she very much needed right then.

Out on the lawn she spotted a flash of golden light. Then another, near the bench under the mulberry tree.

And yet another, in front of the trellis that masked her gardening shed.

"Look, Marsh. Lightning bugs. This is the first time I've seen them this year."

He looked where she pointed, but he didn't say anything.

And all too quickly he turned back to her. They regarded each other through the soft darkness, as the crickets sang and the lightning bugs flared and vanished over the grass.

At last he asked, "What did your mother have to say?"

When he asked her that, she got that scary, hollowed-out feeling a person can get looking down from a high place, no matter how sturdy the barrier against falling might be. There's always that question: What if I *did* fall?

And on this subject, the danger of falling was very real. She wasn't sure how to begin, didn't know how much to tell him about what her mama had said to her.

The truth would hurt him.

And yet, she did believe in the truth. She believed that there should always be honesty first, especially between two people who just possibly might decide to spend their lives together.

Marsh chuckled, but it was a bleak sort of sound. "That bad, huh?"

"No. No, of course not."

"Come on. What did she say?"

"Well, in the end, she said she loved me and to call her if I needed anything."

He grunted. "Why is it I feel as if you haven't told me a damn thing?"

"Oh, Marsh..."

"Just get it out. Please."

She felt terribly defensive—and she had to stifle the urge to go on the attack, to demand to know why he hadn't told her about talking to Rayanne that afternoon.

He said her name, prompting her and somehow seeming to criticize her at the same time.

"Well, it wasn't very pleasant, all right? She and my father, they don't like that you're staying here, they don't like it at all."

"Afraid of what all their old neighbors are thinking?"

"No. No, I don't think that's it. I think...well, they're just worried about me, that's all."

He made a low noise in his throat. "At the mercy of That Troubled Bravo Boy all over again."

She wanted to deny it, but she couldn't, not without telling an outright lie—one he would instantly recognize as such.

"My parents don't know you, Marsh. They never did. They never gave you a chance. And I'm sorry that they didn't."

He looked at her for a long time. At last he muttered, "They had their reasons, I guess. They wanted the best for their daughter. And they knew damn well that the best was the last thing you'd get if you hooked up with me."

"Marsh. They don't know you. They never did. When they do, they'll change their minds."

"Think so?"

"I know so."

"You sound pretty sure of yourself."

"I am. When it comes to your fine character, I have no doubts at all."

That did it. All the hardness left his expression.

He felt for her hand again. And when he caught it, he gave it a tug. She came out of her chair. He guided her around, passing her hand from his right to his left, his chair scraping the patio tiles as he turned away from the table, so that she could stand before him. He pulled her nearer, opening his thighs. She slid into the space between them.

She could see the tenderness—and the desire—in those wonderful dark eyes. She knew he would pull her down to him, that he would kiss her. And, oh, she did want his kisses.

But now was the time, before the kisses started, to ask about what had gone on with Rayanne.

"Marsh?"

"What?"

"My mother said Rayanne called her, and that Rayanne had talked to you today, that she had told you she was going to call them."

He gave the smallest of nods. "That's right."

"You might have warned me."

"I might have. Maybe I should have."

"I wish you had."

"Sorry," he said, though he didn't sound especially contrite.

"Was she...was Rayanne harsh with you?"

He shook his head. "She offered me lemonade. And

she told me how much your family means to her, that you're like a daughter to her and Kim's like a granddaughter. Then she said she felt she had to tell your parents that I was staying at your house.''

''You don't sound angry at her.''

''Why should I be? I think she's a good woman. I think she did what she believed was right.'' She saw his smile, a flash of white through the darkness. ''I'm not too crazy about that living room of hers, though.''

Tory let a low laugh escape, and the sound of it surprised her. It was husky, that laugh. It told the truth about what she was thinking—of getting her mouth on his. ''She had it redone a couple of years ago. It's blinding, isn't it? All that white.''

''Like being inside a giant marshmallow—a giant gold-trimmed marshmallow.''

She laughed again, the same husky, hungry-sounding laugh.

He let go of her fingers and took her by the waist. A lovely shiver went through her at the feel of his hands on her, his palms riding the outward curve of her hips.

He whispered up into her face. ''You sounded pretty sure a few minutes ago, when you said that your folks will change their minds about me.''

''I am sure.'' And she was. Her mother's doubts were nothing to her. She believed what Marsh had told her, about his life in Chicago, about the business he owned there. On the question of whether or not he was who he seemed to be, Tory felt utterly confident. She had seen into his heart years and years ago.

Yes, he might have changed in some ways.

He might have fallen out of love with her. He might have grown up—he *had* grown up. And the man he had become was not the malleable boy she had once held in her arms out at Ten Mile Flat.

But at some basic level he remained her old love. At the level where honesty and trustworthiness lived, he had never changed.

He slid his hands upward, over her rib cage—and higher, so his palms skimmed the side swells of her breasts. She trembled with longing.

"Come down here."

She came down, first bending to him as their lips met and then slithering lower still, until she was on her knees on the patio tiles and he was bending over her, kissing her with all the heat and longing, all the wonder and passion, with that incredible, overwhelming intensity that made her sigh and moan, that turned her inside-out.

His tongue did things to her tongue. And his hands...his hands were loving hands. She didn't remain on her knees for long. Soon enough, he was pulling her up again, settling her across his lap.

They went on kissing. His fingers found their way inside her blouse. He had her bra undone and he cupped her breasts, one and then the other, tugging on her nipples, making them ache in such a lovely, delicious way.

She should have called a halt. She knew it. They had an agreement, and the agreement was not supposed to include sex, not for right now. For right now, they were supposed to be getting to know each other on other levels. They were supposed to be...

Oh, she could not think. Not when he was kissing her. Not when his hands were doing the incredible things only his hands knew how to do.

His warm palm skimmed upward under her skirt. And then his finger was sliding beneath the elastic of her panties, at her hip, moving under and around to the place where her thighs joined.

She moaned into his mouth. Their tongues danced together. And down below, his fingers were doing what they shouldn't be doing. Her body was rising, gathering toward completion. His tongue plunged into her mouth, making the same silky, thrilling motions his fingers were making below, evoking powerful, undeniable responses. Her whole body felt as if it was shimmering, pulsing…

The wave of pleasure crested. And then it broke. She shuddered and would have cried out, but he kept his mouth on hers, drinking in the sounds of her fulfillment.

She went lax with a long sigh, and he cradled her close against his heart.

The crickets sang. And from the mulberry tree, an unseen bird let out one haunting trill of song.

Marsh whispered, "Forget the damn agreement. Marry me now."

She sought his eyes through the darkness, her heart crying, *Yes!*

But she didn't say the word. She hesitated, doubts rising.

Maybe they should wait. Play out the agreement, give themselves another week or so to be a little more certain about what they shared together, a little more sure that what they'd found with each other all over again might actually last a lifetime.

And then there was Chicago. She and Kim would have to move to Chicago, to leave the home they loved and the life she'd worked so hard to build for them.

She hesitated.

It was a grave error.

But she didn't recognize it as such until she had done it and had no way of taking it back.

"Here," Marsh said softly.

She let out a low, bewildered sound. "I...what?"

"Let's get you put back together."

"Oh." She looked down at the open front of her blouse. "Good idea." She shifted around and he helped her to get everything buttoned back up.

Then he took her by the waist and gently guided her off his lap. "We might as well go back inside, don't you think?"

She stared at him. "But I..."

His eyes were hooded, hard to read. "What?"

"Well, Marsh. You just asked me to marry you, to marry you right now."

He stood. "And I shouldn't have done that."

Now she was looking up at him, feeling lost and confused, wondering where she had gone wrong. "You shouldn't have?"

"We made an agreement. I'm willing to stick with it."

"But you—"

"Tory." He sounded tired all of a sudden. "Let's just leave things as they are. All right?"

"Well, but I think that we—"

"Leave it."

She didn't want to leave it. She wanted to talk about it. At length.

But it was very clear that Marsh had done all the talking he was willing to do for one night.

He turned and went inside. She stood there in the darkness for a few minutes, listening to the crickets, watching the gleaming gold flares of the lightning bugs, feeling a bleakness inside herself, a sense of missed connections.

Forget the damn agreement. Marry me now.

She should have listened to her heart, should have instantly cried out, "Yes!"

But she hadn't.

And she couldn't shake the feeling that she'd made a big mistake.

Chapter Fifteen

In the guest room, Marsh lay awake very late that night. He was thinking about Tory. About the way she'd avoided answering him when he'd asked her to throw over the agreement and marry him immediately.

About the way he kept pressuring her.

That *was* what he'd been doing: pressuring her. Trying to get into her bed, using sex as a means to make her see things his way. Up until tonight, that had seemed like a perfectly reasonable way to proceed.

He laced his hands behind his head and stared at the ceiling fan turning slowly above him. He was thinking that maybe he hadn't come that far from the messed-up kid he'd been ten years ago, after all.

He'd kept pressuring her. But she *hadn't* taken him into her bed.

Instead, it had been way too much like the old

days—not the back seat of his car, but close enough. Both of them fully clothed, going at it on the back patio.

And then, afterward, he'd just laid it on her: "Marry me now."

Smooth going, Bravo. Really cool move…

He watched the fan blades go around some more.

They had an agreement. And she was keeping it with class and a great attitude. It couldn't have been easy for her, listening to her mother say all the things he knew damn well her mother must have said about him. But she'd dealt with her mother. And after an initial reluctance for the sake of his feelings, she'd been straight with him, later, when he'd demanded to know what her mother had said.

She was a hell of a woman. And the least he could do for her was to hold to the agreement, too.

He *would* hold to it, from now on.

It wasn't going to be that easy, for her and Kim, to uproot themselves and start over again in Chicago. He couldn't blame Tory for hesitating at the prospect of such a big change. He couldn't expect her to just leap at the chance to walk away from the good life she'd always known.

He needed to back off a little—starting with keeping his hands to himself from now on.

It would only be a week or so, anyway.

Then Tory could take that test and they could start planning how to make all the changes that would need to be made.

The next day, Marsh arranged to have his father's freezer and kitchen cleaned out by a couple of women who ran their own housekeeping service. He drove out to the house and let them in at ten, unlocking the house and also the shed, so they could get to the freezer in there, and showing them where the trash cans were, so they'd know where to put everything.

The electricity was still on, which was good. The weather reports had predicted a high of ninety. They could run the window air conditioner in the kitchen, so they wouldn't have to swelter—at least not while they worked inside the house.

Before he left them, he found a paint-spattered aluminum ladder and climbed to the roof. He discovered that it had been patched, recently, near the place where the watermark had formed on the front room ceiling below. There'd be no need to call a roofer, after all.

He also went into his father's bedroom, where he knew the old man had kept his shotgun. He found the weapon on the floor, on the far side of the bed. It wouldn't do to leave it there, for some petty criminal or crazy kid to find. The house *was* isolated. And a break-in was always a possibility.

He took the shotgun with him into town and got a hundred dollars for it at a pawn shop. He tossed the ticket in the wastebasket on the way out the door.

Over the past few days, he'd rethought the idea of turning off the power and the gas. Houses left without heat didn't do well in the winter months. Pipes could freeze, things like that. So he went over to the electric company and to OK Natural Gas one more time and arranged to have those two services left on, the bills to be sent to him in Chicago.

At a little after one, he went back to the house. He paid the two women and wheeled the full trash cans out to the road where they'd be picked up the next day. Then he locked up the house and drove away, relief manifesting itself as a feeling of lightness, a feeling that he could forget what he didn't want to remember. At least for a while.

There should be no need for him to visit the house again until cold weather came and he had to get the heat turned on—or until he'd made some kind of decision about what the hell to do with it.

The next night, Friday, he got Tory to call the girl down the street to come and keep an eye on Kim. He took Tory out to dinner in the city and to a movie after. He kept the talk casual, told her a few war stories about life behind the wheel of a stretch limousine.

She asked about his apartment in Chicago, about what it was like. He took that as a good sign. He explained to her that it was a full thirty-six-hundred square feet, but that it was still pretty much bachelor digs, not really designed for family life.

He made it clear to her that he was open to buying a house in a good suburb and told her he was looking forward to taking her and Kim to his cabin, which was on a small lake about thirty miles from Chicago. She said she'd very much enjoy a visit there.

They got back to the house at a little after midnight. Once the baby-sitter had left, Tory asked if maybe he'd like a last drink before bed.

He took a pass on that. He gave her a quick, chaste peck on the lips and told her good-night.

The next day the Red Hornets lost their game, three

to five. Kim was glum on the drive home, but already she was planning a big triumph for the team at the final tournament, next weekend. The Red Hornets, she declared, would kick butt in the tournament.

"You're gonna be really proud of me next week, Daddy," she told him that night when he tucked her into bed.

"I'm proud of you right now," he said, bending to kiss her forehead, smelling the now-familiar scents of bubble gum bath oil and spearmint toothpaste, thinking that he would have been staying with his daughter and her mother for two full weeks come Tuesday.

Before next Saturday's tournament, it would be time for Tory to take the test.

And then, as soon as school was out, Kim and Tory could join him in Chicago. They could all live at his apartment for a while. And he and Tory could start looking for a house. They'd want to be settled in a good neighborhood by the time school started up again in the fall.

Kim would miss her friends, but she would get through it. She was young. It wouldn't be that hard for her to adjust, to make new friends and get accustomed to a new life in a new town.

"Good night, Daddy."

"'Night, Kim..."

He rose and left her to her dreams, trying not to think of her and her "very best" girlfriends, Alicia, Ivy and Sophie, all in a row, arms hooked together, running across the soccer field to join the practice drills.

Sunday, Tory wanted to attend services at the Methodist Church not far from the university, the church she'd been going to all her life. Marsh wasn't much of a churchgoer, but he agreed to tag along, since Tory seemed to want it so much.

At church, what he'd been dreading finally happened: they ran into a few people who'd gone to high school with them, including Bob and Stefanie Avery and their six-year-old son and baby daughter. Everyone said how good it was to see him back in town again. And if they were wondering what was going on now between him and Tory, they were too tactful to ask.

And he and Tory weren't telling.

Not until later in the week, anyway. Not until she took the test.

Something was wrong, and Tory knew it.

Something had been wrong since that night out on the patio, that night when they'd talked about what her mother had said. That night when she'd ended up on his lap doing the very things she'd promised them both they weren't going to do.

Marsh was...different, since that night. He was cooler. He kept his distance. Oh, he was always kind, always attentive. But since that night he didn't put his arms around her. He didn't try to kiss her the minute they were alone.

He didn't try to kiss her much at all, to tell the truth. He gave her quick little pecks on the lips—good-night pecks and see-you-later pecks. The kind of pecks a woman might get from a fond relative or a longtime friend. It was really starting to bother her, which she knew was a little unreasonable of her, since the whole point of this time together was to focus on things other than passionate kisses.

Sunday night she decided to talk to him about it.

But when she asked him if anything was bothering him, he said there was nothing.

And what could she say to that but, "Are you sure?"

He said he was positive.

She let the subject drop—for right then.

But she tried again on Monday evening.

"Marsh, it really does seem like something is wrong. Are you sure there isn't something bothering you?"

He said, "There's nothing. Don't worry."

She didn't give up—not right away. "But in the last few days, you've been..." *Say it*, she commanded herself. *Just go ahead and get the question out of your mouth.*

And somehow she did. "You...well, you don't try to kiss me anymore. You keep your distance, whenever we're alone."

He reminded her of what she already knew very well. "I thought that was the idea, to keep the kisses to a minimum, since kisses somehow always seem to lead to other things."

She was pretty sure she knew what he was thinking. The same thing she was thinking. About the other night on the patio. And she felt a little ashamed, to be pushing him about kisses now, when she obviously couldn't stick to her own convictions once he was touching her.

Then he said, "Have you checked into that pregnancy test?"

She had. "I bought one already. Saturday afternoon, when I did the grocery shopping."

"When will you take it?"

"I'm due tomorrow. The instructions say it's 99 percent accurate from the first day of a missed period."

"Tomorrow, then?"

She nodded. "Yes. Tomorrow, we'll know."

She thought of all the ways their lives were going to change. And she realized she was ready to make those changes. Together, with Marsh.

The agreement *had* been a good idea. Now, as soon as they were sure about the baby, she could say yes without hesitation.

Tory woke the next morning feeling glum and bloated. When she sat up, she recognized that heavy, aching feeling lower down: cramps.

But no. It couldn't be…

She checked. And she found that her suspicions were correct. Her period had started. Tory stared at the telltale red stains on her panties and could hardly believe what she saw.

Just to be certain, when she went to the bathroom, she took the test, anyway. Within minutes the results confirmed what her body had already told her.

There was no baby, after all.

Chapter Sixteen

Marsh waited until Kim walked out the front door on her way to school before he asked Tory if she'd taken the test.

She nodded, her mouth slightly pinched and her blue eyes solemn. He understood a little of what she must be feeling. The baby was going to mean big changes, big challenges, for all of them.

He was about to reach for her, to pull her close, to stroke her silky hair and tell her that it was all going to work out okay.

But before he could do that, she said, "I'm not pregnant, Marsh."

He knew he must have heard wrong. That one word: *not.*

Not pregnant.

That couldn't be right.

She was still talking. "My period started this morning. Right on time. And I took the test, just to be sure."

His throat felt like hard hands were squeezing it. But somehow he got out, "And it was...negative?"

"Yes. Negative."

"No baby?"

"That's right."

He stared at her, feeling sucker-punched—and wondering what the hell was the matter with him.

It was all to the good, that there was no baby. Better for everyone. Wasn't it?

"Marsh? Are you okay?" She put her soft hand on his arm.

He pulled away. "I'm fine."

"You don't seem—"

"I said I'm fine."

"All right." She looked hurt.

She *was* hurt. He had hurt her. Jerking away from her touch, barking at her when she only wanted to reassure herself that he was okay.

Of course he was okay.

Why the hell shouldn't he be okay?

Everything had worked out for the best. There would be no big adjustments for anyone to make—well, there would be some. He'd want to work out some sort of visitation schedule with her. He intended to spend time with Kim.

But the wedding was off.

Uprooting her and Kim, making them start all over in Chicago—that wasn't going to happen.

There was no baby.

He couldn't believe it.

No baby.

Why the hell did he feel as if someone had died?

"Marsh," Tory said. "Marsh, would you…do you want some more coffee?"

Coffee. He should have known she would offer him something to drink right then. He might have smiled, if he hadn't felt like the damn world had just ended—which was absurd.

The world had not ended, and there was absolutely no reason for him to feel that it had.

"No, thanks."

Tory didn't know what to say next. She felt so… sad. And he seemed sad, too. But he wasn't admitting it. "Marsh, I…"

"What?" He gave her a hard look, a look she read for what it really was: a form of self-protection.

"I…"

And right then she knew.

It came to her just the way she'd always heard a major insight came to people. In a blinding flash. That was what it felt like—a thousand-watt light bulb switching on in her head.

Everything fell into place for her.

She—why, she loved him!

She loved him as much—no, *more.* She loved him more than she had loved him ten years ago. The two weeks they had spent together had accomplished what she'd secretly dreamed they might do. They had led to love again.

At least, for *her* they had.

"What?" he said again.

Well, there was only one way to find out if maybe Marsh could love her, too. She said, "I love you, Marsh."

He said nothing.

She gulped. "I...did you hear? What I said?"

He nodded.

"Marsh. Will you please say something?"

"It isn't necessary."

"It...what?"

"Tory. You don't need me now. You've got a good life, and so does Kim. You'll manage just fine without me dragging you off to Chicago to start all over again."

This was not going as she might have hoped. Not at all. "But, wait. I'm willing. To go to Chicago."

"It's not a good idea."

"It's not?"

"No," he said with finality. "It's not. You've got a good life here, and I don't plan to drag you away from it."

That was all he would say about it—except that he would leave tonight, if he could get a flight. "I'll stay, watch Kim, until you get home from the shop. And I'll try to be back for Kim's tournament Saturday. You and I can talk more then."

"Talk more?" she asked, sounding like an idiot. But was that so surprising, that she sounded like an idiot? She certainly *felt* like an idiot.

For the second time she'd offered to make her life at his side—wherever that might happen to be.

And for the second time he had refused her.

"Yes," he said. "We'll need to discuss visitation rights. And child support. I'll set something up. If you don't need the money right now, you can put it aside for later."

"For later."

"Right. For college. We can just set up a trust fund. Whatever."

"Whatever," she echoed, not knowing what else to say.

When she got home from the shop that night, he had his bags all packed. He said that he and Kim had already talked. "I've decided I'll come for certain, on Saturday, for the tournament—if that's all right with you."

"I think it's a great idea." She'd tried to inject real warmth into the words. She'd been giving herself pep talks all day, telling herself that she *would* adjust to the fact that Marsh didn't love her, that the important thing now was for them to build a good working relationship as Kim's parents.

He said, "And I was also thinking I'd stay over, until Sunday, so you and I could have a chance to talk about Kim. I'll get a room at a hotel."

She just ached for him right then. The poor man. So sure he would no longer be welcome in her house. He ought to know her better than that.

"A hotel room isn't necessary. Please. Stay here."

"No, I—"

"I mean it. Stay here."

"If you're sure…"

"I am. And where *is* Kim?"

He shrugged. He really did look miserable. ''She's not very happy with me. We talked—or *I* talked. As soon as she got the message that I was really leaving, she ran to her room and slammed the door.''

Tory folded her arms over her chest. ''She's in her room now?''

''Right.'' He frowned. ''Tory, it's okay. She's upset and she—''

''Wait right there.'' She spun on her heel.

''Tory, I said it's—''

''It is most certainly *not* okay.'' She said the words over her shoulder as she marched down the hall.

Kim was lying on her bed, staring at the ceiling. She bolted upright when Tory shoved open the door.

''Mother. You *could* knock.''

The stereo was playing. Tory strode over and punched a button. The stereo went silent.

''Mama! I was listening to that.''

''Get up and come kiss your father goodbye.''

''I don't want to.''

''Sometimes, young lady, you have to do things you don't want to do. This is one of those times.''

Kim's mouth trembled. She cried, ''He's *leaving.* He's *really* leaving.''

''He's not, either. He's coming back on Saturday, for your tournament. And he's already planning ways that you can go and spend time with him.''

''It's not the same. I want him *here.* I want us to be a family.''

''Well, sometimes in this life you just don't get what you want. That's no reason to hurt someone who loves you very much.''

"He doesn't love me. If he loved me—" Kim cut herself off. She was looking past Tory, at the doorway. At Marsh, who must have followed her down the hall.

"Tory," he said, pain twisting his fine features. "Let her alone."

Tory gave her daughter a long look, a look only a mother knows how to give.

The look was enough. Kim leaped from the bed. She flew to Marsh. He caught her in his arms. She was sobbing by then. "I don't want you to go, Daddy. I *hate* that you're going."

He held her close, whispered, "I'll be back. Saturday."

"Promise?"

"Cross my heart."

Kim and Tory both walked him out to his car.

All the rest of that week, at the shop, Tory kept telling herself that she was going to have to accept the fact that Marsh did not return her love. She'd made her own feelings painfully clear to him. She'd told him she was willing to live where he lived.

And he had turned her down flat.

Accept it, she kept silently instructing herself. Marsh doesn't feel the same way that you feel. He stayed because of the baby. And now that the baby isn't coming, he wants to be free.

But her heart would not listen. Her heart kept reminding her of how good it had been between them—at least until that night on the patio. How they had grown closer, every day. Of how he was with Kim.

The man was born to be a father.

He *should* have more children.

And, oh, if she had anything at all to say about it, those children Marsh should have would be *her* children, too.

Her heart simply would not be silenced.

Her heart demanded that she give it one more try.

Marsh called on Thursday to say he would be flying into Will Rogers Airport at eight Saturday morning. He'd join them at the soccer fields, since Kim's first game was also at eight.

On Friday, Tory called Rayanne from the shop.

"Oh, Tory, honey. I am so glad you called."

"I have been pretty angry with you."

"Well, I figured that out all by myself. How many days has that man been gone now?"

"Since Tuesday night."

"So that's at least two days you have not called me to look after Kim."

"I've managed." She'd been picking Kim up after school and taking her to the shop with her.

"Tory, honey, I had to do what I felt was right."

"Well, and you did it, didn't you?"

Rayanne didn't answer that one. She just went right on. "Audra called me back after she spoke with you last week. She didn't seem to think her call had changed your mind about things one bit."

"It didn't. Rayanne, I love Marsh. I want to marry him."

"Oh, dear."

"I need your help, Rayanne. I need you to believe

in me and believe I am doing the best thing for myself and my daughter.''

Rayanne took a long time to speak. At last, she grudgingly confessed, ''Well, I guess I have to admit, I've had a few second thoughts about that Marsh Bravo, since I went and talked to him, face-to-face.''

''Second thoughts?''

''He does present himself well now. Like he's made something of himself. And he *was* a gentleman when I talked to him. A lot of men wouldn't have behaved half so well.''

''Yes. Marsh is a wonderful man. And are you going to help me?''

Rayanne sighed. ''You know, there's no reason that Kimmy can't just come on over to my house this afternoon.''

''Will you help me, Rayanne?''

Tory recognized the quality of the silence that ensued. She knew Rayanne was studying her rings. Finally Rayanne spoke up. ''What is it that you want me to do?''

Saturday Marsh arrived at Griffin Park in time to watch Kim make two vital saves. The ending score for that game was three to four, in favor of the Red Hornets. They had another game at two. The Red Hornets triumphed again.

That meant one more game, for the championship, on Sunday afternoon. Marsh got on his cell phone and managed to change his plane reservation to late Sunday night.

At six, he took them out to dinner at Othello's, an

Italian place near the university where the atmosphere was dim and cozy, and Dean Martin and Frank Sinatra tunes played in the background.

After dinner, at home, Kim wanted to get in a few games of U-No. Her doting father obliged her. They played for two hours. It was well past nine when Tory finally told Kim to get her stuff together. It was time to go next door.

Marsh waited until his daughter had gone to her room to get ready before he demanded to know why Kim was going to Rayanne's on that night of all nights.

Tory gave him a tender smile. "I really thought it would be better if you and I had a chance to talk without the possibility of any interruptions. We can call Rayanne at seven in the morning, and she'll send her right back over."

He frowned. But he didn't say anything other than "Oh."

Kim had her hands full by the time she was ready to leave. She had her pajamas and her favorite pillow and a little zippered vanity kit with her toothbrush and toothpaste. She kissed her father and then Tory walked her next door.

When Tory got back, Marsh was waiting in the front hall. "Does Rayanne know? That I'm here?"

"Yes, Marsh. She knows." She shut the door and locked it and then she turned back to him. "She's decided you're not so bad, after all."

"She has?"

Tory took a step toward him. "That's right."

He backed up.

Tory kept coming—and she kept her mouth shut. At least until the urge to offer him a cold drink could pass.

"Marsh," she said. And then didn't know what to say next.

He must have realized he was backing up, because he stopped and planted his feet apart, a man determined to hold his ground. "Tory, what is going on?"

She made herself keep coming, until she was standing right in front of him. She wanted to cry. She wanted to turn and run. She wanted to throw her arms around him and hold him so tightly he could never get away.

She said, "I meant it, what I said last Tuesday, Marsh. I love you. And I want—"

He grabbed her by the arms and shook her. "Don't." His eyes burned into hers. "Damn it, Tory. You don't have to do this."

"Oh, yes, I do." She spoke with grit and pure determination. "I love you. Maybe I've always loved you. Maybe I never stopped, in ten whole years. Oh, I don't know if I stopped loving you—or if the love was always there, a tender thing, sleeping, waiting for you to come back and wake everything up again.

"I don't think it matters, if I stopped, if I didn't stop. What matters is that I *do.* I love you now. That I want to make my life with you."

He held her very still, his fingers digging into her arms. And he looked…struck speechless.

Was that a good thing?

Maybe she had scared him. Maybe he was afraid to tell her that he did not love her. Maybe he thought she might do something terrible as soon as he dared to say such a thing.

What was that old saying?

Hell hath no fury like a woman scorned.

Is that what he thought? That as soon as he scorned her love, she'd go crazy or something?

She hastened to add, "But I...I *will* understand. If you don't feel the same. I'll understand. And I'll accept it, I promise you. I just...I have to know for sure. I just want you to tell me. Do you love me?"

He swore.

It was hardly what she'd been waiting to hear. She wrinkled her nose at him. "That is not much of an answer, Marsh."

He moved then. He yanked her to him, hard and close. And he whispered desperately against her hair, "I...I *wanted* the baby, Tory."

"Oh." She held him tightly, as tightly as he was holding her, and she pressed her lips together, swallowed. But the tears spilled over, anyway. "Oh, I know you did."

He went on, holding her so close, whispering his heart's secrets into her ear. "The baby was like another chance, to do it the right way. To be there when you needed me, to show you that I was...good enough to be with you. To be your husband. To be...a father to your children. I just *knew* you were pregnant. I was absolutely certain of it. And then, when you *weren't,* I couldn't believe it. Couldn't accept that it wasn't going to happen just the way I had it planned." He kissed her hair, then cupped her face in his fine hands and made her look at him again. "You're crying." He smeared at her tears with his thumbs. ''I never wanted to make you cry.''

''Oh, Marsh. Don't be sorry. Not for these tears. These tears are *good* tears. They mean that you're talking to me. They mean that we're finally getting things out in the open.''

''Oh,'' he said, looking so handsome and so confused. ''Is that what they mean?''

''Yes. And Marsh?''

''What?''

''I have to ask you—that night, after my mother called, out on the back patio...''

''What about that night?''

''Well, you did change, after that night. When I asked you before, you said that you didn't, that nothing was wrong. But *something* was wrong. I know that it was.''

He gave her the sweetest, most rueful smile. ''I was taking the high road. I'd decided I should quit trying to seduce you into saying you'd marry me.''

''You did?''

He nodded. ''By then, we only had a few days to go, anyway. I was so certain you were going to *have* to marry me.''

''But I didn't *have* to. I didn't *have* to at all, Marsh. I *wanted* to. I still *want* to.''

''You're sure? You're absolutely certain?''

''How many times do I have to say it? Yes. I am certain. I am 100 percent positive. I want to be your wife. I want to be with you, in Chicago. Anywhere. It doesn't matter. As long as we're together, you and me—and Kimmy.''

He kissed her nose, rubbed away more tears. "I've got an idea..."

"What?"

"I have a great manager at Boulevard now. He can almost run the place without me. I'm ready to branch out. What do you think about the city? Think they can use a new limousine service there?"

She hardly dared to breathe. "You mean *Oklahoma* City?"

"Yes. What do you think?"

"You mean...we could live here, in Norman, after all?"

"I'd have to go back and forth, to Chicago, at least for a while. But maybe, whenever you can manage it, you and Kim could come with me..."

"Marsh. You haven't said it. You made *me* say it over and over, but you still haven't said it to *me*."

He smoothed her hair. And he kissed her wet cheeks, one and then the other. And he said, "I love you, Tory Winningham. Will you marry me?"

Before she could get the word, "Yes," out of her mouth, he was kissing her. He scooped her high against his chest and he carried her off down the hall.

The next day the Red Hornets lost to a team called the Rockets. Kim was disappointed, but on that particular day, nothing could dampen her spirits for long.

Her mother and father were getting married. And Grandma Audra and Grandpa Seth were coming home for the wedding. And next week, her mama had promised, they would go looking for her maid-of-honor dress.

And soon—oh, she just knew it—she would have thc little sister that she'd been longing for.

Epilogue

On a Sunday morning in late September, Tory came out of the bathroom carrying the little white wand from the pregnancy test. Her husband was waiting, sitting up against the headboard, all his hopes and dreams shining in his dark eyes.

"Well?"

She held out the wand.

"Blue," Marsh said.

They stared at each other.

He said it again, "Blue. That means it's..."

She nodded. "Positive."

With a low sound of pure joy, he reached for her. They held each other tight.

A moment later she moved in his arms, getting herself settled close against his heart. He whispered of his love. And she whispered back. Promises of forever.

Promises that both of them knew now they would keep.

At ten, they went to services at the Methodist Church, where they ran into Bob and Steffie Avery and invited the couple and their kids over for dinner the next Saturday. Bob and Steffie said they'd love to come.

In the afternoon Kim and her friends had a party at a theme park in the city to celebrate Alicia Sabatini's tenth birthday. Kim went to Alicia's at noon, carrying a big present in bright birthday paper. She wouldn't be home until after five.

"When should we tell her?" Marsh asked, as they watched her run up the walk to her very best friend's front door.

Tory leaned across the console for a quick kiss. "It's early yet. I think we should wait a while—a few weeks, anyway."

Alicia's front door opened. Kim disappeared inside.

Marsh started up the car. They were halfway back to the house when he suggested quietly, "I'd like to go out to my father's place. Would you come with me?"

She put her hand on his arm. "You know I will."

They went back home for the keys, and then they headed out east.

About halfway there, Tory asked, "Why now? Because of the baby?"

He sent her a quick, warm glance. "At least partly,

I guess. But mostly because I know who I am, now. I'm ready to deal with whatever we find in that back room."

The house was locked up securely, undisturbed since the last time Marsh had been there, in May.

It was a hot day—predicted to hit somewhere in the midnineties. The first thing they did once they got inside was to turn on the window air conditioners in the kitchen and in Blake's bedroom.

Then they went to the office.

Marsh got the air conditioner going in there, too. As soon as the cool air began to circulate, bringing relief to the stifling, dim room, he turned to the computer. His wife was already pulling open file cabinets and peering inside.

The computer started right up, but as soon as it got to the Windows screen, a prompt appeared demanding a password.

Tory glanced his way and saw the problem. "Great. Let me guess. Your father never mentioned any password to you."

"My father never mentioned this computer to me, let alone a password."

Right then, he heard his father's voice, on the day before the old man died.

Your big surprise, Blake had said. *Your big, glittery surprise.* He'd used the word *surprise* a lot that day, and always with way too much relish....

Marsh typed in the word *surprise* at the prompt.

Seconds later he was inside.

"How did you do that?" Tory demanded.

"Guess I knew the old man a little better than I thought I did." He began clicking icons.

She came up behind him. "What's in there?"

"A file with my name on it." Marsh clicked the file open. In it, his father had stored information about Boulevard Limousine and about its owner, Marshall Bravo.

"Where did he get all this?" Tory wondered aloud.

"Off the Internet mostly, from what I can see. He's cut and pasted whole pages from our Web site."

"He found you on the Internet?"

"Looks that way." He closed out that file.

"What else?" Tory asked.

"Other files, with other names."

"Names you know?"

"Nope." He clicked more icons.

Tory said, "Wow."

Marsh nodded. "Looks like financial records. Spreadsheets. A lot of them." He noticed she held a manila folder in her hand. "What's that?"

"Your father's will." She opened the folder, held it flat for him to see. "Done by a law firm in the city. Notarized." She pointed at the notary seal.

"And?"

"He leaves everything to you."

"Everything meaning...?"

"That, he doesn't say. It's just the basics. Explains how he's to be cremated and that all the expenses of his last illness are to be paid from his estate. Everything else goes to you."

"His *estate,* huh?" Marsh made a dry sound in his throat as he flipped through the screens. "He's got every damn penny he spent in the last five years accounted for, it looks like. Amazing. Of course, it doesn't say where he *got* his pennies. Figures just appear in the 'credit' line, with no explanation.''

''We should take this with us when we leave,'' Tory said, holding up the will.

''Okay.''

She set the will on the desk and went over to the bookcase stacked with newspapers and tattered tabloid-type magazines. After a few more minutes of flipping through computer files, Marsh got up and joined her.

''Mostly California newspapers,'' Tory said. There were copies of the *Los Angeles Times,* the *San Diego Union-Tribune,* the *San Francisco Chronicle* and the *Sacramento Bee.* They read a number of headlines from years and years ago, glanced through several of the dusty, dog-eared magazines.

Then they found the scrapbook.

It was sitting all by itself on the top shelf—a fat, once-white photo album, now yellowed with age. Marsh brought it down.

Taped to the front of it, in bold letters on plain white paper, was one word: Surprise.

What they discovered between the covers of that yellowed album almost defied belief. It was a tale of wealth and privilege, of murder—and of a death that had not really taken place. A tale of a stolen baby boy, and of a fortune in diamonds paid in the futile hope that the glittering treasure might bring that baby home.

And on the last page, held on with layers of transparent tape, was a key.

The next day Marsh and Tory drove up to Oklahoma City to visit a certain branch of a large national bank. Marsh carried his briefcase with him and conferred with one of the bank's officers, providing the fellow with his father's death certificate, his own identification, and the notarized copy of his father's will that Tory had found in the file cabinet.

The officer would not allow Tory to accompany Marsh into the vault, so she sat in a wing chair in the waiting area. It didn't take Marsh long. He was back at her side within five minutes of disappearing behind the huge steel door.

He held the handle of the briefcase in a tight fist. ''Let's go.''

She didn't say a word, just got up and followed him out into the muggy September afternoon.

The ride back home was very quiet. She didn't ask. He didn't tell.

When they got into the house, he hefted the briefcase onto the table, undid the latches and laid the thing open. Along with the papers he'd taken to the bank, she saw a black velvet jeweler's bag.

''Oh,'' she breathed. ''Oh, no…''

''Oh, yes.'' Marsh picked up the bag and carefully spilled its glittering contents onto her breakfast table.

Tory felt slightly sick. She groped for Marsh's hand. He gave it to her, wrapping her fingers in warmth and strength—in steadfast and undying love.

"What now?" she whispered.

"We found the diamonds. Now we try to find a way to bring that stolen baby home."

* * * * *

Marsh Bravo may have had
the best of intentions, but how
could they find the stolen baby?
And could *he come home?*
The answers begin
in Silhouette's Single Title,
THE BRAVO BILLIONAIRE,
coming in September....

HARLEQUIN "SILHOUETTE MAKES YOU A STAR!" CONTEST 1308
OFFICIAL RULES
NO PURCHASE NECESSARY TO ENTER

1. To enter, follow directions published in the offer to which you are responding. Contest begins June 1, 2001, and ends on September 28, 2001. Entries must be postmarked by September 28, 2001, and received by October 5, 2001. Enter by hand-printing (or typing) on an 8 ½" x 11" piece of paper your name, address (including zip code), contest number/name and attaching a script containing 500 words or less, along with drawings, photographs or magazine cutouts, or combinations thereof (i.e., collage) on no larger than 9" x 12" piece of paper, describing how the Silhouette books make romance come alive for you. Mail via first class mail to: Harlequin "Silhouette Makes You a Star!" Contest 1308, (in the U.S.) P.O. Box 9069, Buffalo, NY 14269-9069, (in Canada) P.O. Box 637, Fort Erie, Ontario, Canada L2A 5X3. Limit one entry per person, household or organization.

2. Contests will be judged by a panel of members of the Harlequin editorial, marketing and public relations staff. Fifty percent of criteria will be judged against script and fifty percent will be judged against drawing, photographs and/or magazine cutouts. Judging criteria will be based on the following:

   - Sincerity—25%
   - Originality and Creativity—50%
   - Emotionally Compelling—25%

   In the event of a tie, duplicate prizes will be awarded. Decisions of the judges are final.

3. All entries become the property of Torstar Corp. and may be used for future promotional purposes. Entries will not be returned. No responsibility is assumed for lost, late, illegible, incomplete, inaccurate, nondelivered or misdirected mail.

4. Contest open only to residents of the U.S. (except Puerto Rico) and Canada who are 18 years of age or older, and is void wherever prohibited by law; all applicable laws and regulations apply. Any litigation within the Province of Quebec respecting the conduct or organization of a publicity contest may be submitted to the Régie des alcools, des courses et des jeux for a ruling. Any litigation respecting the awarding of a prize may be submitted to the Régie des alcools, des courses et des jeux only for the purpose of helping the parties reach a settlement. Employees and immediate family members of Torstar Corp. and D. L. Blair, Inc., their affiliates, subsidiaries and all other agencies, entities and persons connected with the use, marketing or conduct of this contest are not eligible to enter. Taxes on prizes are the sole responsibility of the winner. Acceptance of any prize offered constitutes permission to use winner's name, photograph or other likeness for the purposes of advertising, trade and promotion on behalf of Torstar Corp., its affiliates and subsidiaries without further compensation to the winner, unless prohibited by law.

5. Winner will be determined no later than November 30, 2001, and will be notified by mail. Winner will be required to sign and return an Affidavit of Eligibility/Release of Liability/Publicity Release form within 15 days after winner notification. Noncompliance within that time period may result in disqualification and an alternative winner may be selected. All travelers must execute a Release of Liability prior to ticketing and must possess required travel documents (e.g., passport, photo ID) where applicable. Trip must be booked by December 31, 2001, and completed within one year of notification. No substitution of prize permitted by winner. Torstar Corp. and D. L. Blair, Inc., their parents, affiliates and subsidiaries are not responsible for errors in printing of contest, entries and/or game pieces. In the event of printing or other errors that may result in unintended prize values or duplication of prizes, all affected game pieces or entries shall be null and void. **Purchase or acceptance of a product offer does not improve your chances of winning.**

6. Prizes: (1) Grand Prize—A 2-night/3-day trip for two (2) to New York City, including round-trip coach air transportation nearest winner's home and hotel accommodations (double occupancy) at The Plaza Hotel, a glamorous afternoon makeover at a trendy New York spa, $1,000 in U.S. spending money and an opportunity to have a professional photo taken and appear in a Silhouette advertisement (approximate retail value: $7,000). (10) Ten Runner-Up Prizes of gift packages (retail value $50 ea.). Prizes consist of only those items listed as part of the prize. Limit one prize per person. Prize is valued in U.S. currency.

7. For the name of the winner (available after December 31, 2001) send a self-addressed, stamped envelope to: Harlequin "Silhouette Makes You a Star!" Contest 1197 Winners, P.O. Box 4200 Blair, NE 68009-4200 or you may access the www.eHarlequin.com Web site through February 28, 2002.

Contest sponsored by Torstar Corp., P.O Box 9042, Buffalo, NY 14269-9042.

SRMYAS2

COMING NEXT MONTH

#1417 THE LAST MERCENARY—Diana Palmer
Soldiers of Fortune
Mercenary Micah Steele hadn't seen his stepsister, Callie Kirby, since their forbidden attraction led to a family split. Now kidnapped by a drug lord, Callie was the bait to reel Micah in—and he came running. But when the adventure was over, would the last mercenary finally claim his bride?

#1418 TO CATCH A THIEF—Sherryl Woods
The Calamity Janes
When Gina Petrillo returned to Winding River for her high school reunion, trouble followed her home in the form of lawyer Rafe O'Donnell. He was sure that Gina had stolen money from his clients. But once he caught his "thief," would the only thing she really had stolen turn out to be his heart?

#1419 WHEN I DREAM OF YOU—Laurie Paige
The Windraven Legacy
The Windoms and Herriots were archenemies for three generations—until Megan Windom met Kyle Herriot and hate turned into passion. But when their investigation revealed the meaning behind Megan's nightmares, they knew their only chance for a future…was to resolve the past.

#1420 ANOTHER MAN'S CHILDREN—Christine Flynn
While Lauren Edwards baby-sat her brother's toddlers, his business partner, Zach McKendrick, stopped by to lend a hand—and wound up lending a little more than that. But a past love and a plane crash had left Zach scarred inside and out. Would this ex-test pilot realize that Lauren's love could heal all wounds?

#1421 HER SECRET AFFAIR—Arlene James
Interior designer Chey Simmons was hired to restore Brodie Todd's crumbling mansion, not his heart. But when he needed help exposing deceptive family members, Chey pretended to be his lover. Would her secret affair soon become a public proposal?

#1422 AN ABUNDANCE OF BABIES—Marie Ferrarella
The Baby of the Month Club
After years of separation Stephanie Yarbourough encountered past love Dr. Sebastian Caine while he delivered her babies—twins! Now, if she would only put her faith in Sebastian once more, double the babies could have double the love.

SSECNM0801